THE PAPER WOMAN

THE PAPER WOMAN

Françoise Rey

Published in Great Britain in 1992 by Nexus
338 Ladbroke Grove
London W10 5AH

First published 1990 by Editions Ramsay, Paris,
under the title *La Femme de papier*

Copyright © 1990 Françoise Rey

Typeset by Avocet Typesetters, Bicester, Oxon
Printed and bound in Great Britain by
Cox & Wyman Ltd, Reading, Berkshire

ISBN 0 352 32827 4

Translation copyright © Nexus Books 1992
Translated by Sue Dyson

NOTE TO THE READER

Reader,

Normally, you open a book and, on the very first pages, you encounter a man and a woman who don't yet know each other, and whom you discover separately. Little by little, you see them meeting, liking each other, loving each other. It's also par for the course, I think, after a few establishing chapters, to come to more intimate, spicier episodes. Stories often end like that, or at least – at a certain stage – include the carnal communion of their heroes, and certain writers excel in this genre of knowledgeably prepared apotheosis.

This book escapes these classical laws of narration, at least as far as its structure is concerned. The woman who is writing is dreaming of, or remembering, her lover (who has perhaps asked her to do so) and meetings which they perhaps had. But her spiritual progress brings her towards ordinary pathways, and little by little it leads her to make a surprise discovery: the discovery of the forest which was hiding the trees.

For it is indeed true that sex leads to all things, including love . . .

And so you will not be surprised that the dedication, which in another work should have featured on the title page, is located at the end of this journal back in time . . .

1

In those days I was a timorous mistress, and you were a conventional lover – too often in a hurry, and too often imbued with that role which you thought was your privilege: handing out pleasures, ceaselessly renewed.

My quest was different: I wanted tender seduction, not frenzied attacks. I was tired of your blundering dynamism, and my reserve disappointed you.

We had met, and came to belong to each other without further ado. We were preparing to leave each other, equally directly, if you can call it 'leaving each other' when all we had was an episodic and – as I have already said – not very harmonious relationship . . .

Was it the sudden no doubt far-sighted sadness of losing you without making any effort, or perhaps the pride of showing you that, on paper at least, I knew how to prove my audacity? What bizarre, immodest impulse compelled me to suggest, and then write, this first letter to you?

My forbidden love,
 My companion of pleasure,
 My friend in moments of laughter,
 Come: I shall lead you into the musings of a fine, daydreaming woman with a tender heart and an unoccupied

7

cunt. I shall take you with me because you shall be my inspiration, and also because you seemed interested by the proposition. I shall do my best to be readable, but if in a little while I am not, you mustn't blame me – it will be your fault . . .

Give me your hand, your thickset hand, bigger and warmer than mine, your hand which has never had the patience to learn to be a little gentle . . . Follow me into this warm, intimate, almost darkened room where incomprehensible chance brings both of us, without thinking to explain ourselves to anyone, without thinking of the passage of time. And with no reservations; for, can you imagine it, we are not there for what ordinarily unites us, and takes the place of complicity for us! The proof is that I have abandoned myself to pleasure in an exquisitely soft chair, absolutely vast for one person but a little small for two. And I'm on the telephone. I don't know who it is I'm phoning, and I don't know what they're saying: it doesn't matter. I reply 'Mmm yes!' from time to time, because the speaker's voice has a powerful soporific effect, and also because you are there, sitting on the ground at my feet, and you are caressing my legs through my tights, very carelessly, with the tips of your fingers, as though you were thinking about something else. It's a light touch rather that a caress, but my God it's good: I could spend hours like this, listening to your fingers amusing themselves as they run across the conspiratorial nylon mesh, across my ankles, my calves, my knees . . . And the hollow behind my knees, I'm not even going to mention that! I think I even moaned down the telephone.

How skilled your hands are this evening. I can feel them wandering wonderfully over my body. Here is one now, daring to climb higher under my skirt . . . No! Back down it goes . . . It reaches my foot, and that's not bad either, I can feel its effects at the other end of me. Is it possible to bring a woman to orgasm by stroking her foot? Ah – here comes another hand. This one is bolder, without appearing to be, and it slips gently between my thighs. I very much want to give it a welcome, to part my thighs a little, but my

8

skirt is too tight. It's a delicious torture to want to open yourself and to be prevented from doing so. The fetters end up becoming as exciting as the caress, and yet the caress is becoming more and more precise . . . I haven't the courage to move so as to pull up my skirt, because that might spoil everything . . . But neither do I have the courage to force my body to remain immobile. It begins to twist and turn in a way which I would term indecent, for my head is still cool even if the rest of me is starting to warm up. And I stay there, listening to this inexhaustible telephone conversation, and looking down at my skirt which is stretched to the extreme (I'm sure it's going to split!) because my knees are mad with the desire to pull apart. As for your hands, which have long understood their power, they are definitely abusing the situation . . . You see, you are making me hollow the small of my back, and my buttocks are contracting in the strangest way. It's reaching a critical stage.

A quarter of an hour ago, I was unaware of the fact that I had a cunt. And now I can't forget it. It is red hot inside my knickers, and I can feel it moving all over the place. Like a mouth suckling, like a living animal breathing, like a heart beating. I have a little engine there at the base of my belly, which is pumping away all on its own. It is vibrating, wet, it cries out for a more direct touch, a more concrete caress. I am clouded by my shape, which takes life beneath your fingers. Suddenly I become aware of my emptiness, my voids, my folds . . .

How can I spend most of the time without realising that I am divided, down there, by a voluptuous fur muff which only asks to be opened, a very long, sopping-wet crack, running from my belly to my arse, which – needless to say – is also taking part in the celebrations? I can feel it palpitating too, at the same time as the other hole; they understand each other very well, those two, when it comes to obscenities, I can assure you. I have nothing more to say – they are beating in unison, contracting and dilating together, dancing an infernal sarabande for me: look, we've got to do something . . .

Too bad if my skirt is crumpled. I pull it up as best I can with one hand (the other is still on the telephone). Ah! I've got a funny little belt of rumpled material around my belly, but my legs are free. Whilst I was lifting my buttocks to relieve my constriction, you have grabbed hold of my tights. Wonderful! You know how to take advantage of your chances. I am breathing more easily . . . That's just an expression though, because at the same time my breathing also starts taking liberties. And so I am no longer mistress of anything, neither my pelvis, which continues to move backwards and forwards with great immodesty, nor my lungs, which start doing Lord knows what. Which is really practical when you're on the telephone! My God! That's true – there's still my knickers! Why do I put so many clothes on in the morning? Mind you, they don't seem to hamper you much: you're playing with the elastic around the legs. You've slipped your two index fingers under the little bit of lace, and with the tips of your fingers you're following this signposted route. Ah! I positively adore the symmetry of your movements. You start off from the hollow of my groin, and I can feel your nails running through my pubic hairs, and you move round under my buttocks. Then you climb up again. If you stretched out your fingers a little, you could touch my cunt. I'm sure it would swallow you up: it's uncontrollable. Or my arse, even? But you don't want to – it visibly doesn't interest you: in spite of all the advances my body is making to you, you remain very much master of the situation, of rhythm and movement.

I must be muttering incomprehensible nonsense on the telephone, because I'm asked to repeat what I have said. No, stop. I really don't know what I'm saying any more. I have to sit up, prop my back against the armchair and cross my legs in a dignified manner. Instead of that, I have gone so far to meet your hands that I am sitting on the very edges of my buttocks, right on the edge of the chair, with my torso almost lying flat in its depths, and my legs! Oh! The horror of it! No one could be more consenting, more offered . . . I would die of shame if I tried to measure the space between my feet, where you are crouching. The most horrible detail of all is that my feet aren't even flat on the floor, but are stretched out, and arched on the tips of my toes. They know instinctively that they are taking part in my offering, and that I am even more open.

No! What a sight I must be! It's incredibly exciting . . . Fortunately there's still my knickers to safeguard a few of my secrets. But not for long, because you are amusing yourself by pulling the gusset first to the right, then to the left, a gesture which shames the remains of my modesty and completes the job of inflaming my cunt. But take my knickers off – take them off and look at me! Look at me palpitating: I can't take any more . . . Do you see? What do you see? Do you see this mouth calling to you, demanding you imperiously? You know, it moves of its own accord – it's nothing to do with me, I'm irrelevant! Right in the depths of my loins there is something which is growing and breathing in and becoming irritated. No – don't put your fingers there! It's too sensitive, and you wouldn't know how to touch it in the right way. It's an explosive clitoris, and I can feel it stiffly erect: if you brush against it, I shall come and then I'll feel completely empty because I shall not have had you inside me.

You know what I need. Your prick, right away. And to think that I no longer imagined this fellow as having a prick. How can you forget things like that? All I have to do is imagine it, and my cunt is tight, small, maddened . . . Come, come! Show it to me, unbutton your flies! You're moving away from me maliciously, and escaping from me. But I have feet too, you know. If I place my foot gently there in between your legs, and caress your balls, you won't move away any more, will you? I can feel your big fat prick through the fabric of your trousers . . . Feet are wonderful things – they understand an awful lot . . . Ah! I've caught your fly-button. No, I shan't put down the telephone. If I hang up, I feel as if the spell will be broken . . . I've got you! Button, zip fasteners, with one hand, that's just about OK, but all the rest . . . But you'll help me . . . Don't you want to give me one? Well? Look!

That's it: my right hand has left your trousers and is now taking part in an impossible exhibition. The situation is too urgent for me to have the time or the strength to take off my knickers completely. But as they aren't too tight, I'll prepare a way for you, shall I? At the side. Right or left — have you any preference? Well? Ah! You seem to capitulate. You are lowering your trousers and your underpants. You're still on your knees in front of me. Wow! It's great, your prick! I'm in love with it. I want it, I want it madly. I'm going to guzzle it down, pump it, swallow it whole . . . I'd like to touch it, but if I stretch out my hand I'll have to let go of my knickers, and that will close the way to you. Ah! I'm going to wedge the telephone receiver against my shoulder. That way, I have one hand for the knickers, and one for your cock. I've caught hold of it now: it's not so very timid . . . Come closer, closer! You enjoy keeping me on tenterhooks; that's very bad. You shouldn't play like that with a woman who's all stretched out, all wet and giving herself to you so hard! I can feel your cock moving in my hand. I am terribly hungry. I feel as though I am very small and ravenous, and the feeding-bottle is there, only ten centimetres away. I am at once a little innocent animal, tortured by an imperious need, and a Bacchante, untrestrained and lewd.

My body, which has just taken power, begins unparalleled obscenities, and will ignore me if I try to govern it. My right leg is celebrating anarchy, laid across the arm of the chair; the other would like to do the same on the other side, but it's a bit too far. And yet, if I try very hard . . . My fingers, which are pulling aside my knickers, are venturing as far as the entry to my cunt; I am making a royal road for you: it's smooth and soft, wet through, and it reacts quickly, I want you to believe that! Your cock wants it too, and here it is at last . . . careful, gently, just the end, if you please? You have placed its hot tip between my lips, and are enjoying being on the edge of me as I demand you. A little further, come on! And as you are making as if to move away, I move briskly forward to meet you and engulf half your prick, with something like a cry of joy which comes from my entire being at once. But you are still very stoical, and you set a firm, gentle rhythm which is very regular and unbearable.

I let go of the telephone. My left hand has taken hold of your prick at its root, the better to appreciate its stiffness and its movements; to accompany, encourage, accelerate or slow them down – I don't know any more. The right hand, which I have been holding back for so long, has flown away and touched the detonator: a clitoris so excited that I could cry. There is a sea, an ocean of pleasure sending enormous waves of pleasure right through my cunt, my entire vagina, and nothing can change the rhythm of this ebb and flow, even if I beg 'harder!' or 'faster!' I feel your prick invading me, then moving out again. I know its shape, its volume, with millions of nerves at once I recognise its gentle, rounded head, and its cleft, the padded cap of foreskin which disrobes it, along the length of the shaft. I know that you will draw back almost until it comes out of me, and I shall be alarmed, anxious to the point of pain, and then you will come back, even stronger, bigger, stiffer. I push to meet you, and I breathe in to hold you there. It's an extraordinary ballet, to a music which both of us understand, and my entire body is lifted up by this symphony. Look! By dint of trying, my left foot has reached the other arm of the chair . . . I feel as though I am divided right down to the soul. I am completely yours – if you left me now, it would kill me! Can you feel how I belong to you? One hand clenched tight in your hair, and the other madly stroking my clitoris, absolutely abandoned to your possession, all my mucous membranes welcoming you, submitted to your law; all I desire is your prick fucking me, and I want that passionately. Take, take me, take everything, fuck me and look at me, listening to me coming to you . . . It's coming from a long, long way away: I was a cavewoman, and you were taking me even then, and I held your buttocks as your enormous battering-ram penetrated me . . . You have all power over me, fuck, fuck, come and fuck me, give it to me, screw me, you are going to kill me and bring me into the world . . .

It was an orgasm worthy of a prehistoric era . . . No doubt

I cried out things which you like to hear, and the animal you had unleashed in me howled without really wanting to, and the whore I love to become from time to time knew very well what she was saying.

It was good, very good, thank you. And how was it for you? Ah! That's another story! Next time, I swear I shall pump away at you until I drain you dry, and I shall make you spit your flame, and maybe I shall even make you cry out . . .

Well, I can dream, can't I . . .?

2

I delivered that first letter to you by hand, rather than entrusting it to the post, as if I wanted to assume the entire responsibility for it. When you gave it back to me a few hours later, there was a gleam in your eye. I returned your gaze heroically: my reward was the interest which I read in your eyes . . .

'Is that a list of instructions?' you asked me, pleasantly. And at that moment I knew that from now on it would be easier for me to domesticate your good will.

'A very incomplete list . . .' I replied.

'In that case, I await the rest of it with impatience!' you said.

A new relationship was born between us, and how much more exciting it was . . . Your curiosity flattered me. I took it upon myself as a duty not to disappoint you.

It was one day – the most miraculous of all – when I was thinking of you without daring to expect too much. It was miraculous, because you fell into the hollow of my bed, which a long daydream had just warmed up in the sunlight of my fantasies. The light of your green pullover lit up the bedroom, left gloomy by the rainy morning. The light of your yellow-gold eyes lit up the whole of me.

All at once, I wanted you. You got undressed, and I wondered if I would have the strength to wait for you — the desire for you made me writhe about sinuously underneath the sheets. When you joined me, you were a little cold, but you found me burning hot, and it is true that I was burning. How soft your skin was, how terrifying your body . . .! You turned your back to me; my belly marvelled as it moulded itself to your backside, and I caressed you like that, pressing my breasts against you with their erect nipples, my navel, my pubis, my thighs. I intertwined my legs with yours, wrapped them around you, and my cunt, which opened as I embraced you, crushed itself against your skin . . . My arms were around your waist, and my hands began to move about impatiently on your belly. I found your prick, although all I could see of you was the broad base of your neck, your expectant back, and that insolent arse which sometimes made me regret that I was a woman . . .

Your prick, captive between my fingers, trembled a little, but it was in no way as rebellious or as vindictive as I had learned that it could be. And my hands were astonished at this new languor, and my body was irritated, bridling and disappointed . . . You heard me thinking, you said something about being tired, or perhaps having the flu. The word provoked me: suddenly I wanted to make you feverish . . .

May all the whores of the earth be my inspiration! Shall I be able to find the gestures, the words, the rhythms which will transform you into a panting, lust-crazed male? Will I be able to invent the caresses, rediscover the art of loving prized by the old courtesans who made men's pricks rear their heads to the heavens? This so sweet, so unusual passivity, which I have so often hoped for from you in vain, and which you are offering me today, is an act of defiance, a whiplash in the face of my feminine vanity and my desire. What a contradiction! I don't want you to be indolent and abandoned any more. I dream of you being proud, wild, demanding, with a prick like a marble column, and I shall worship at this monument, and allow myself to be impaled whilst I close my eyes, torn and overwhelmed, martyred, marvelling, torn apart between pain and pleasure. At heart, I am a devotee of phallic religions; I shall become their priestess, celebrating your cult with my hands, with my mouth, with my cunt and my arse and my entire body. I want to give you such a hard-on that it will remind you of those fabulous bestiaries where man and horse were one.

Have you understood the depth of my resolve? You are lending yourself to my caresses with a good will, and in your eyes I can read a curiosity which encourages me . . . Do you know that I have decided to make you the most powerful man in the universe? Look carefully: watch as this monstrous prick grows between your legs. It will make you the equal of the faun, the satyr, this god hidden in the foliage of a mythical forest. Whenever he came out of the bushes, his prick preceded him by so much that it sowed terror in the bellies of the women, and envy beneath the tunics of the men . . . I shall caress you for as long as it takes. I have eternity before me; I am the first woman in the world, the most beautiful, the most skilful, the first slut, and this story of the serpent which people tell, well, I can confide in you that it has been strangely garbled. I'm going to tell you how it happened: you were there before me, the first and only man, my mirror, my double, or nearly. When I touched your difference, it was moved. I wanted to charm it, so I stroked it for a long time with my hand, and then with both my hands. I stretched it, I kneaded it, massaged it, masturbated it; and the more it swelled up, the more it fascinated me. And as for the serpent, I invented it . . . And here we are again, for a remake which is more recent by so many centuries, and yet so similar to the original version.

I am kneeling between your legs, your servant, your humble slave and yet your mistress, and my hands recall millenia of knowing how to tease, how to please. They run over you, separate, come together . . . One on each of your

17

thighs, they climb up at the same pace and are now under your testicles, emphasising their roundness by cradling them in a gesture of prayer or offering; your balls seem made to lie in the hollow of my hands. And yet 'lie' seems a rather inadequate term, for I can feel them moving in my palms, hardening a little, as though they were ripening under the effects of a powerful alchemy. And your shaft too is ripening as I roll it between my fingers. I let go of it and move back down to your thighs, forcing them apart a little; then I return to it, first of all wandering through the intimate furrow which divides your buttocks. I catch hold of it, grip it very tight, and enjoy sliding it up and down with movements which visibly electrify it. But I want it to be even bigger, more engorged, more imperious. Mentally, I call to my aid all the lewd geishas of Japan, all the masseuses of a legendary Orient; I call up the little Chinese whores with their delicate fingers, the streetwalkers of Hamburg, Amsterdam, Berlin, the girls who suck men off without the trace of a scruple, and whose world is full of demoniacal filth, the Saigon women who masturbate men and allow themselves to be buggered, all the vice-girls, the hookers whose occupation is men. I appeal to their knowledge, their science, their art . . . What did Calypso, the curly-haired nymph, do to keep Ulysses on her island for so long, to put fire in his balls? She was a sorceress who knew incantations and formulae. At her altar, the hero of endurance was there, a prisoner, stupefied by the rod which she had made spring forth at the base of his belly. I shall become Calypso for you, I shall make you forget everything, except the horrible torment of a disproportionate prick, swollen fit to burst, throbbing in the quest for deliverance.

You are twisting about too; you want to fuck, but I'm beginning to learn the way to keep putting things off. I have taken you into my mouth, but you can scarcely bear to stay there: I am irritating you with my tongue and my lips, and my hands are masturbating you at the same time as I am sucking at you.

18

I am going to milk you, Ulysses, Tristan who drank the philtre and whose penis remained erect until death . . . I am going to pump you, draw out your liquor, but not yet . . . I would like you to be even more maddened, even more demented! Let the rutting madness of the great African apes, tall negroes and all the giants of creation rise up within you . . . Do you see this elastic band on the bedside table? I am going to knot it around your prick, strangle it until the congestion becomes unbearable, until your cock threatens to explode. Three turns around the base – does that feel as if it's gripping you tight? Look: it no longer belongs to you, it's dancing a wild dance. How swollen it is! This is the first time I have seen you get wet. You see, it's an enormous fruit engorged with juice which is flowing out in the sunshine. You have a vegetable prick: a formidably tortured, knotty, scarlet, obese, delectable root. Look how aroused and arousing you are, like that! But I'm more eager for your own pleasure than for mine. You feel for me, you want to mount me, to screw me, and your prick is so sick with desire that it is leaping about against my belly. No! I shall get astride you; I shall make love to you, fuck you. You surrender. You can do no more with this gigantic hard-on which asks for nothing but to bury itself anywhere, in a hole, to rub itself and burst forth. I shan't touch myself for a single second. I am the complete mistress of the situation; I ease myself gently down on to your ramrod, very gently, and move back up again. I have steel springs in my thighs, and a vacuum cleaner in my cunt. Don't move! I can fuck you like this for an hour if you wish. Don't move, I tell you. Feel everything to the full: your prick is buried in my cunt, right up to the hairs, sucked, aspirated, spat out very slowly, very, very slowly. For an hour, if you want . . .

No, in a few seconds you abandoned the struggle. You arched your back and closed your eyes. At that moment, I felt so proud that I forgot to put my finger on my clitoris . . .

You were a little vexed, considering that you had just lived through a sort of defeat, and neglecting to celebrate my sort of victory . . . You odious fellow, my dear love, when will you understand that your surrender was sweeter to me than your stiffness, and that I keep the memory of your pleasure within me like the memory of a moving confession?

3

'Very interesting, very, very interesting . . .' You wore
your typical smile – like an old, ironic little boy – and
your entire large body was full of impatience. You seemed
to be forcing it to remain immobile, but it took a com-
mendable effort.

'So? When?'

This elliptical question, and the sparkle in your wicked eye,
and all the fire which I sensed within you made me burst
out laughing.

'Wait, wait a while!'

That very evening, I wrote you my third letter.

Dear dirty old man,

What can still interest you in a woman you have undressed,
whose modesty has capitulated under your gaze, moaned at
your caresses, cried out in your embrace? Beyond all her
tenderness, all her kisses, all her gifts, all the words she dared
to speak, all the gestures she dared to make, what remains
to a good-hearted mistress who wants to captivate her lover
still further?

There remains one secret, which, of course, he desires: the
secret which she never had the audacity either to speak or

21

to do, which passes furtively beneath her eyelids, which she keeps obstinately closed as pleasure approaches, which, in times of delirium and fever, haunts the head of this good woman who is in other respects so reasonable . . .

You want images, words, stories which will make you all the harder because you know the author. And since I don't (and mustn't) have any other expectation, here you are:

There came one evening when our tender complicity and our shared love of strange things and fantasies, and perhaps also a few glasses of champagne, led us further than I could have said: for you had sometimes explained to me that 'sex toys' and props had never excited you; and as for me, my reserve (I forbid you to smile) had stopped me from making any kind of provocation . . .

But that day, I was coming back from G. where I had pillaged my grandmothers' wardrobes, as I always did when I went home. I brought back some extraordinary loot, including a selection of *belle époque* underwear. As I was going through the contents of my suitcase for you, you said it was a pity that it didn't include the famous suspenders which drove men wild in the fifties. Because that was the first time you had ever shown any interest in a licentious object, I took it upon myself to demonstrate to you that our grandmothers, in their time, hadn't had any reason to envy these creatures in the Paris-Hollywood films which made our fathers' pricks stand erect.

First of all, next to the skin, they wore a chemise, a little tunic which was too short to hide the essentials, and whose straps seemed to have been carefully designed to slip nonchalantly down over the shoulders. The one I slipped into had lace on the neckline, which just managed to tease the tips of my breasts. At first sight, the pantaloons looked more decent, since they hid the thighs and were tied at the knees by two apparently very modest cords. The corset was very rigid. I asked you to lace it very tightly at the back. It hollowed my back, but accentuated the graceful curve of my hips, which was already expansive anyway. This made me look like a woman from another age, quite at sea in the twentieth century. As for my bosom, the stiffness of the boning, which emphasised it with a double shell of ribbons, exaggerated its roundness and arrogance, and I'm sure you immediately wanted to bite into these apples, offered to you in their frilly basket. All dressed up like this, I could have passed for one of those naughty turn-of-the-century engravings, which made so many venerable moustaches tremble with desire. As for you, you seemed amused, perhaps a little softened, but certainly not trembling . . . So I showed you the hidden obscenity of my knickers. I put my foot on a chair and said to you: 'Look!' Against the whiteness of the linen, my pubic hair seemed darker. With one hand, I parted the obliging vent of my underwear to give you a really good look, and with my fingertips I also pulled apart the more intimate vent which divides the base of my belly. And – already aroused – you contemplated this telescopic, voluptuous sight, the white encircling the black, and the black serving as a frame for the pink, which was more alive, more pearly, more quivering. My fingers enjoyed their role as tour guides. They opened up a path for you into this delicate, juicy fruit, as welcoming as a peach which has just burst in the sun, as vibrant as a shell whose secret depths have just been forced open . . .

You stood up; you had a strange look about you . . . You took hold of my shoulders, and turned me towards the mirror set into the wardrobe. 'You look, too!'

For a long time I had accustomed you to being obeyed; I looked. What a delicious torment it is to catch sight of oneself in debauchery! I am standing in front of the mirror and my clothes expose rather than cover me. My nipples are erect, darkish red, and make double punctures in an embroidered border, and in the opening of the pantaloons, which my leg on the chair causes to gape as wide as you could wish, you can make out a funny sort of animal, half fur, half living flesh. You are behind me, watching me watching myself, and the light in your eyes contains something which makes me almost afraid . . .

I turn away from our double reflection to look at you and

search for the proof of that emotion which gives a yellowish tinge to your devil's eyes. Your prick is not forked, but it is swelling your flies in an eloquent way. How quick you are to discard your clothes! Now you are naked, with a wild prick at the base of your belly, drawing an arrogant exclamation mark across our image in the glass. You catch hold of my arm determinedly, sit down on the chair and draw me towards you, backwards.

'Open wide and tell me what you see.' As you speak you make an imperious movement which forcibly impales me on your ramrod. With your legs, on which my thighs are resting, you part mine . . . What do I see? Oh! Can I find the words? I see a woman torn apart, her cunt gaping wide. I see your balls under my arse, and your prick sticking into my cunt, which is so wet that at each movement you can hear a little splashing noise . . . I see my maddened hands trying to open myself even wider. I see your hands, guiding mine to your balls and demanding caresses. I see my wild dance, which engulfs you and throws you back with the rhythm of a well-worn piston. I see your hard, massive prick. Now I see it, now I don't, now I see it, now I don't . . . Who invented mirrors? Who first had the idea of discovering himself, enjoying his image, masturbating in front of the mirror, fucking with his reflection? Ever since Narcissus, there have been cheval mirrors in the brothels and today I can understand why as I savour the double pleasure of the actor and the voyeur, the disturbed pleasure of watching a filthy film of which you and I are the stars. The expression which takes over my face is all the more terrifying to see than the play of my cunt, sucking your cock. This is really me, this creature concentrated at the limit of pain, with her mad, imploring eyes, her mane of hair racked by the winds of a tempest, her mouth begging, saying 'yes' and 'no', and 'again'. Is this my head: the head of the mare bitten by the stallion, thrusting back her neck as she thrusts our her backside? . . .

Joy makes me leap upwards one last time, my back hollowed and my thighs stretched to breaking point. Only the tip of your cock is left in my cunt, shaking me with a few last shivers . . . And as I am about to breathe a sigh of relief, marking the end of the round, I feel you, still rather rebellious, looking for a more secret way into me . . . I have no time to protest really, because already you have found my arse, and you are ill-treating it with the head of your cock, which is a horrible nosy parker and is rummaging about all over the place. You pull apart my buttocks with both hands, and force the way, which surrenders and I cry out. That's it: you're in. I'm stuffed full to bursting. Pain and pleasure are mingled, and in spite of myself I am twisting about on your shaft. The pleasure which had not completely subsided resumes its rights; I am so full of you, with this rending sensation that I must expel you, which makes me push, and desire you further, deeper, which makes me tighten my arse and push down as far as I can on to your prick. My cunt is inhabited by a demon. I am yours more intimately than ever. I give you all of me, and I reach that state of dementia which mixes gold with filth and love with shit. You alone chose the pathway into my body which is nothing other than a sewer, and the surrendering of the ultimate barriers – so go on, pump into me that way too and forgive me if delectable divagations rise within me, marrying pornography to scatology. You give me a furious, divine desire to shit, and that's perhaps what it is to climax – a consenting continence, resolved and organised until it bursts forth.

The mirror is still there, and I take the measure of it. I lift up my eyes to my reflection and see myself impaled like that, the emptiness of my cunt. One of my holes is too full, the other too deserted . . . And my feverish fingers will not gratify this immense void which you have hollowed out there, by invading me elsewhere . . . It is instinct and need more than method, which makes me find that candle on the dressing table. You, you see nothing. You are still sitting down and my back masks the mirror. You are only preoccupied with my arse which is sucking at you, and my comments which you are begging for. And so I am going to tell you: I am fucking my own cunt with this whore of a

25

candle which I happened upon, and I am working hard to overturn the meaning of that ridiculous expression 'hold a candle', which is supposed to mean being present without taking part. To hold it, I swear that I am holding it well, and my God, I know a way to take part too. With my eyes, fascinated, I follow the incredible rhythm of this wax cock which my cunt is swallowing and spitting out, and I feel deep within me, through an elastic, vibrant partition, my candle bumping against yours. Ah! I'm not short of a flame, believe me . . . You could say that that's the spark which ignited the powder . . .

The explosion was of Dantesque proportions. I'm pretty sure it was quite a success from your point of view, too . . .

Tell me, if my grandmothers are watching me from somewhere, do you think that it would please them to recognise their clothes? . . .

4

It was immediately after then that things were turned upside down. Each of us became a sort of work of art which each of us had set our hearts on working at meticulously.

From my letters, you had gleaned how patience and application can bring dividends. And as for me, they had convinced me of the pleasures of a healthy violence, well orchestrated, accepted and even sometimes expected . . .

When we met each other, we progressed with an infinite curiosity through the gestures, words and situations which we had yet to discover. We had the fevered passion of collectors, the ambiguous wisdom of limiting our joint preoccupations to sensual pleasure alone.

Henceforth, we loved each other enough to live out a disordered, strange, dreamlike story together . . .

A day came when I could no longer refuse you anything. Because she had clearly demonstrated a more than flattering interest in you, and because she didn't leave you indifferent either, on that famous Wednesday I found myself alone with her, waiting for you. It was the first time I had conjugated that verb, 'to wait for you', and yet it was so familiar to me in the first person plural . . . I had accepted out of a desire to please, out of cowardice, out of curiosity, and also out of

27

wisdom. For I knew perfectly well that one day or another, in whatever way, you would make love with her.

Paradoxically, jealousy made me consent to, and even organise, this uneasy threesome. All jealous people will tell you that they owe their most terrible sufferings to their imagination. And so I would prefer to see and even act rather than imagine. And I did not find the idea of taking part repugnant; I told myself that you would never quite know to which of us you owed your orgasm – her or me: already that doubt was a consolation to me. And I had resolved that I would not only be acquiescent, but effective.

When I recall that day, I feel a real delight in seeing your embarrassment when faced with both of us. With me, she was first of all silent, almost hostile. When you turned up, she became frankly confused. And even you were very embarrassed and talked a lot, waving your arms about, grimacing and laughing; and I liked your way of being timid, which I knew very well, but which scarcely reassured *her*. For a moment I was tempted to allow myself to fall prey to a diabolical inertia, to watch . . . But no! It would have been clumsy to disappoint you when it could be so easy to dazzle you. I was courteous enough to let you set the ball rolling. You settled yourself on the settee, putting your arms round us as we sat on either side of you, and declared: 'I am a sex object, use me as you please.' I was on your right, but it was she who heard your heart beating. Her languid attitude annoyed me; I wanted her to be more Latin, more bronzed, with longer hair, more passionate and more authoritative. And yet, when that little slut put her hand on your fly, for one painful moment I was tempted to slap her . . .

But after a few minutes, emulation took the place of complicity for us: she had only her left hand free, and I had only my right. Together, we got past your trousers and your underpants and, sincerely, I don't know now which of us it was who took hold of your prick, which our caresses seemed to have excited as much as you could desire.

A little game began: she took you into her mouth, then withdrew. I did the same, spurred on by the look she had

28

given me. Then it was her turn, and mine again. The manoeuvring lasted for a long time: you abandoned yourself shamelessly, and, as you had laid your hands on our heads, you even orchestrated our comings and going in a very rhythmic way. I felt a double and in some ways very ambiguous pleasure: the pleasure of sucking you, and of eating after her. Your prick was different, it had the same shape and the same consistency, the same evocative power, made the same little jerky movements as I titillated it with my tongue, but it tasted different, and it slipped between my lips in a different way. Because it was licked and desired by another woman, it became the symbol of a wager, but also the magical, voluptuous hyphen between our mouths and our saliva. She and I drank from the same fruit, and suddenly I realised that the enjoyment was multiplied three times: the enjoyment we were procuring, that which we were experiencing, and that which we were offering to the Other Woman, the Second, the Rival; each time she allowed it to escape, she saw a bigger shaft come back to her, excited even more by the rival's mouth . . .

Suddenly, I was more eager for her pleasure than for my own: I gave up all the room to her, and she accepted it immediately. She slipped willingly between your legs and knelt there, but remaining sufficiently accessible for me to be able to caress her under her skirt. That's what it's like when you've got an unspoken agreement. And how well women can understand each other sometimes! Her thighs were sweet and smooth when I began to stroke them. I had once loved a woman, and the memory of our mingled embraces was dear to me. My hands began to remember, at the same time as they rediscovered feminine roundnesses, attractions, the elasticity of a skin which was half silk, half velvet, the supple, melting warmth of delicate tissues, the disturbing moistness of her valley . . .

She remained kneeling, with her back to me, but made the task easier for me by a thousand acts of cooperation, parting her thighs, arching her back, offering herself completely to my caress whilst she was lavishing her own, for she was still pumping away at you, and at your feet you had a sort of stack of slave women, one to serve your prick and the other, even humbler, submitting to the first.

I began to release her from her clothes. The skirt came off without any problem; she twisted about so that I could get her knickers off. It was a hot day, and she had bare legs and on her feet she wore beautiful sandals, which added a splash of brightness to the lower part of her unveiled body. She had a particularly exciting arse — round, mobile and sexy. I pressed myself up against her from behind and took hold of her round her waist. How hot she was! She responded to the pressure of my body by sticking out her buttocks, and my hands began to dance a delicious ballet over her, the choreography owing more to intuition than to technique. They slid under her T-shirt, which she wore next to her skin, without a bra; they found her breasts, imprisoned them, evaluated them, teased them. Her breasts were rather small, rather pointed, and how they were trembling! Under my thumbs, I could feel the nipples hardening, moving rhythmically; very gently, I began to brush against them with the flat of my wide-open hands. The pleasure was absolutely shared, and this titillation with the hollow of my hands became so suggestive, so disturbing, that I suddenly discovered I had a tremendous thirst for her. I slid on to her as though she were a guitar, a sensitive instrument which would vibrate with inspired music at the touch of the lovelorn musician. I left her breasts and moved to her hips, taking hold of her buttocks. From roundness to roundness, I let myself go . . . Oh yes! It was more a case of intuition than technique, but from now on, and more than by intuition, the gestures which came to me were dictated by my sole desire, a mad desire to possess her, to overwhelm her, to seduce her, wank her, eat her and drink her, discover the taste of her and her most intimate odour, and blow up a storm in her belly. I became her rival when she ceased to be mine, and I began, in charm and in talent, to surpass that disproportionate shaft which you were still brandishing, and which she was still adoring on her knees before you. You were

30

filling her mouth, and I was rummaging in her cunt. And please believe that my groundwork, a knowing mix of gentleness and violence, was not without effect! She began to stream like a fountain beneath my fingers, and little by little I saw her knees draw apart so as to make it easier for me to carry out my investigations. I touched her with both hands, completely and conscientiously. I opened her up as you open up a juicy midsummer fruit; I let my fingers wander up and down her cleft, and as I passed by I even felt her arsehole, which called out to me, trembling, as I touched it. She lifted herself up a little; she was no longer on her knees, but crouching, and it was easy then for me to penetrate her, very deeply, very symmetrically. I stuck my two index fingers into her cunt at the same time. It was as slippery as if it was covered in oil. And I stuck my two thumbs into her arsehole, which was offering itself to me so insistently. She was hot inside there, as she was outside – burning, delicious, so exciting that I could have howled out loud. I amused myself by pinching and testing the elastic partition which separated my fingers. I slid in and out of her arse with regular, firm movements, and enlarged her vagina with a very slow, very gentle circular motion.

My hands were mad with intelligence, bearing her off whole, since as the pleasure took her over, she became gradually heavier on my wrists. But I was stronger than Atlas at that moment, and the burden which was resting on my arms – a delirious but well-brought-up woman, who did not cry out with her mouth full – was more important that the entire universe. She gave a few rapid, vertical movements – the galloping of a wooden horse on a roundabout – and I was very careful to accompany her in her ecstasy by holding her very firmly, and then she became still, tense, stiff, at the summit of the joy which I had just given her.

In her ecstasy, she had let go of your prick, and I think that's what set off your violent and spicily unpredictable reaction . . . It was your turn to be jealous, and this double power which I suddenly discovered I had, the power of overwhelming and making you jealous of it, filled me with

31

an exquisite pride. But I scarcely had the time to taste my triumph. Already you were taking hold of her, firmly and precisely. You turned her over, sat her down on you, on your stubborn prick, and I discovered myself, without moving, in front of you and at your feet. It was towards you that she was now turning her back, and she was facing me. Her thighs were spread wide apart on you, revealing the disturbing spectacle of your union. I saw your shaft buried deep in her, your balls, slightly crushed beneath her buttocks, and her gaping cunt, soaked and marked by the tide which had just flooded it, pearly, gleaming, hesitating between dark red and the tenderest pink. I gazed at it distractedly, wanting my gaze to burn her, and I'm sure it did burn, for she kept her eyes obstinately closed. That's very impolite, madam – you should always look people in the face! It's very impolite and it's very stupid, for there is nothing more delicious than shame at certain moments. Come on, little sister, open your eyes and watch me watching you. I'm making love to you with nothing more than my eyes. Read in my eyes and on my face what I'm seeing there, twenty centimetres away from me. Decipher my confusion and my desire; my sensual pleasure in watching you like this, a lewd woman, stripped of all her secrets. Your wound is deep, clear cut, precise. The hairs which surround it emphasise it without protecting it. I am learning all the petals of your flower by heart, and the foam on your shell; I know without touching it that your clitoris is erect, irritated. I burrow into you, I record your every detail, I savour you, I leer at you without the slightest scruple. I see the male shoving his piston into you, I see you tightening your cunt on his marble column, and the juice which is escaping from you moistens his balls little by little. It's fascinating and disgusting, and in this spectacle I forget the dimensions of reality, I touch a fabulous universe where life is no more than a coupling, a mythical, millenarian, antediluvian universe. Your sex organs are uncertain molluscs – mussel, razorshell, sea urchin, with marine sap, with slimy, elastic flesh, a strange snail, a viscous slug . . .

I am hypnotised by your nuptial rites; my heart and my

cunt seem to beat together to the rhythm of this ballet, as old as the world. Look at me, little whore, as he gives it to you; little whore who's getting fucked and doesn't even dare to lift her eyelids! Your cunt is open to the four winds and your eyes are closed tight shut on the remnants of an old modesty. Hypocrite, slut, darling – you suffer more from giving yourself than from holding back! If you look at me, if you dare to open your eyes on the humble witness of this intimate, captivating marriage, I shall suck you. Do you understand? I shall suck you and bring you off more surely, more quickly and further than this big cock which is blindly burrowing into your cunt!

All she gave me was a little flutter of her eyelashes, which it was tempting to take for a surrender. I put my mouth on her and drank at her spring. She was as good as a peach, warm, smooth, juicy and perfumed. She smelt of woman and man at the same time, and with the same kiss I embraced both of your sex organs at the same time, for you were still working away at her, lifting her and pulling her down by the waist, according to the rhythm of your whim. I made love with my lips and my tongue, with my teeth, to a strange hybrid creature, male and female; I licked your cock when she left it, and her crack when she came back down and impaled herself on it. It was bizarre and exciting. You tasted of her cunt and she tasted of your cock. You were both wet, soaking, sweating, and I mingled my saliva with your dew, attentive and conquered for the first time by the sounds of marshlands, of water lapping, sucking noises, a whole immodest, suggestive symphony of sticky organs.

She came again, still without crying out, every muscle in her body tensed up and with her belly thrust forward, and that pleasure reunited you and me, who had been separated by the preceding orgasm. In making the same woman tremble at the same time, we had perhaps just achieved a closer communion than if I had been in her place, impaled to the hilt on your prick.

That day, we stayed with that silently signed peace, and parted without giving in to easy pleasure – you, who, as usual, wanted to be a hero of endurance, and I who hadn't even got undressed. We left each other as lovers and accomplices, before this little girl, this good little woman who, having enjoyed us both thoroughly, came to know the unpleasant and disturbing feeling of being surplus to requirements.

5

You were often brutal with me, to the limits of sadism. Taking advantage of your strength and my weakness as a woman – the weakness of a woman in love, which is even greater – you frequently inflicted on me uncomfortable positions, mad rhythms, violent caresses, a thousand little humiliations imposed by the master's hands, and a thousand little humiliations which – as a slave devoted to the point of sadness and pain – I submitted to: a thousand little humiliations which I consented to with the sorrowful, bewildered joy of the Christian martyrs. Which didn't prevent me from complaining or denouncing them, and you always replied: 'Well, take your revenge then!'

Now the time had come.

I had the strangest desire for you – truly a strange desire. I said: 'It's today that I'm going to avenge myself – you're going to pay.'

You made the mistake of replying: 'If you want, whatever you want . . .' You never should have done that . . .

First of all, it was essential that you accepted the rules of the game, absolutely, unconditionally and once and for all. For I knew your false promises of obedience, of total passivity, and your sudden, last-minute revolts, your

35

cheating, your bad faith. I warned you: 'I shall have to tie you up.' Because my voice was a bit different and a little anxious it roused your curiosity (that's your big weakness, curiosity!), and you abdicated all responsibility. 'If you want, whatever your want.'

You never should have done that!

You found yourself torn asunder on the bed, trussed up and tied to the four bedposts. I had brought along little cords for your wrists and ankles, and it was a perfectly premeditated crime. The situation seemed spicy to you; you appeared intrigued, but there was something dark in your bright eyes, an almost stormy light passed through them, and I knew that, somewhere, you were a little afraid. This anxiety was delicious, for it excited me even more than your big naked body, offered up defenceless to my thirst for reprisals.

'You may tremble, for you know, I am going to take you where you have never been, and you will not come back until you are broken, shattered, marvelling, terrified . . . For the first time, I am the captain of the vessel, and I am inviting you to set sail with me, into the storm, into hell . . . I love you as much as this evening I am going to try to hate you, scorn you, use you, reduce you to nothing. I shall make you howl your suffering, your terror, your revolt . . .

'I am switching off the light because I need complete darkness to cast off the moorings, conspiratorial night which will favour my chimera and make of you what I want you to become, and of me what I dream of being for the space of an instant, a dream, a nightmare . . .

'Here I am lying against you, as naked as you are, and first of all in the depths of the gloom I am trying hard to recognise your body, my domain, by using my hands and mouth: for this night is moonless, devoid of all light. I run my hands and lips over you, reading you with my open palms, deciphering your braille with my fingertips. Here is the back of your ear, which is rather short, the deep line etched into your strong-willed chin by the same grimace over so many years; there is your powerful neck and your rounded shoulder, the inner surface of your arm — so soft it seems

36

edible: and that doesn't hinder me. I lick it and bite it. And here again is the underside of your arm, moist and fragrant, whose odour I recognise amid a thousand others . . .

'I am running my fingers over your smooth chest, your young, elastic belly. I am wriggling them underneath your buttocks which fill my hands, overflowing them with firm, springy, dynamic flesh. With my cheek, I feel the warmth of your pubis, the dark frizzy vegetation which is already fenced across by your prick, which starts under my face. How quickly, how well and how strongly your penis leaps to attention! It is perfect: today you must be desperately erect, more than ever; you must become erect as people dance, suffer pain, pray, or cry out. With the back of my hand, I stroke your long, muscular thighs, which are as woolly and soft as two beautiful high-bred animals. I draw their outline, I recreate them, and the shivers I draw from you make you give little moans of pleasure. That's good. Instinctively, you know how to please me and what I am expecting from you. Pay attention, listen to everything I have to say to you, what I want to tell you with my mouth and with my nails which are scratching you slightly . . .

'It's a terrible story. Once upon a time . . there was once a man who complained a little because he was happy. In the darkness, someone patient, someone skilful and demoniacal caressed him with genius, as one might touch a work of art, an artistic masterpiece, a quality piece of furniture, a velvety fruit. And at the touch of the mouth and fingers of this diabolical artist, the man arched his back, lifted up his buttocks, twisted and turned with a nameless lasciviousness, and offered up his swollen prick, with the suggestive bead of liquor at its tip.

'He began to moan more loudly when he felt his balls being licked by a madly inspired tongue, a tongue which was very hot and very supple, but also pointed sometimes; it was a very wet tongue, very all encompassing, unpredictable, knowing, unhoped for. Then he made out the touch of lips on his pubic hair, amusing themselves by separating them, uncurling them, teasing them so slowly, so methodically that he thought he would go mad. The skin of his scrotum felt as if it was burning alive, more receptive than ever, and it felt as though it had contracted, for within the so-cleverly titillated envelope, he felt as though two very dense, very hard nuts were ripening, ready to explode with pleasure . . . And then everything – pubic hairs, skin, nuts – everything disappeared, swallowed up, snatched by a demented, unusually eager mouth; and he imagined himself being sucked, drunk, swallowed right up to his soul, and his maddened prick began to throb with great jerky movements, looking for a cave, a gulf, a hole in the darkness in which to wank itself off and die . . .'

That's how I wanted us to be, with you the delighted, ecstatic victim, humbled through petitions, and myself as the artist, the torturer who promises and does not give in, the demon . . . People say that angels have no pricks; at that moment I guessed that demons don't either, or rather that, along with devilish status, a sulphurous androgyny is also conferred on them. In the thick blackness of that night where you twisted and turned and called out to me, I felt that I was no longer a woman. At some other time, guided by the powerful instinct of my too-empty belly, I would very quickly have sat down on that wild, incandescent prick, which I was holding so very lightly in my hand, and, even though you were tied up, you would still have been the male, the aggressor and penetrator, who invades everything, the arm which profanes and the mouth which spits, and as for me, even on top of you, even though I had freedom of movement, I would once more have been the female, an emptiness to overflow, a hole to be filled, a mouth which you would force and saturate . . .

And yet, that evening, I knew nothing of my organs and my femininity. My cunt was not sounding a parley. It was not waiting for your battering ram to thrust into it. It was not trembling with the desire to swallow you up . . . My entire body had disappeared, and I was a witch, or rather a warlock; my too soft, too hazy contours had flown away, the roundness of my breasts and my hips had been erased, and the throbbing of that marine conch shell at the base of my belly, which lives and breathes and moistens like a mussel, had been annihilated . . . And whilst you were demanding me with voice and movement – a very soft, unaccustomed, submissive, hoarse voice and a movement of the pelvis which lifted you off the bed and laid you back down on it very rhythmically – I was present at this strange miracle which I had hoped for for so long. I saw you become a woman as all femininity left me. Listen well: you were not effeminate, not softened, lessened or pretty. You were a woman with your prick pointing to the sky and your narrow hips, your nervous, hairy legs and your strong arms. You were a woman in your delirium, in your need, in your murmurings and your bonds, a woman because you had submitted to me, because you were pulled apart, a woman because you were tempting, mad, noisy and impatient. You were a woman in the style of the great warriors of Hannibal, a woman like sailors, soldiers, the prisoners who, faced with solitude and a lack of tenderness, seduce the other person in the cell, their companion in the dormitory. A woman like a soldier, prostrate with fear at the bottom of his trench, who prefers to allow another soldier to fuck him to forget death, suffering and squalor. In your ballet of love, in your cries, there was the troubled grace of the heroes of dark, disturbing films: you were the detainee who seeks, on the skin of another detainee, the escape which the midnight express will no longer bring; you were, though unveiled, that creature with hermaphrodite charms whose blue eyes disturbed and seduced a whole generation of cinemagoers, shining in the deserts of Arabia; you were the defeated man, the humiliated man who strikes down his conqueror with an ambiguous look, a kiss on the mouth. Listening to your plaintive song, pressing your maddened flesh, brought to my mind all the refined brutes with their handsome faces, all those virile, muscular, harmonious, masculine bodies, all their movements, all their gestures, all their dances; and as I discovered you had become a woman in their image, I wished that I was a man, and I closed my eyes, and gave way to the marvellous, delicious, abominable dream of being your male lover rather than your mistress. My body now existed only through my fantasy. I became very strong, very strong, and it gave me an amazing hard-on listening to you moving about and moaning in the darkness . . .

Very brutally, I searched for your arsehole. That's what I wanted – your only secret, hidden entrance, as yet never profaned. It pleased me intensely that you should be a virgin on that count, as I would be the first and you would remember it for a long time . . . When you understood what I was planning, you strained to escape, protested, shouted 'no!' again and again, in fevered tones. Oh! How I loved you, how I loved your fear, at that moment, your fear and your distress and your pain! For I penetrated you without taking the slightest precaution, eagerly, furiously, with both thumbs at once, nails together, not much bothering if I grazed you, and even confusedly hoping to hurt you, mark you, signpost my rape with a burning, perhaps bleeding, scratch . . .

Your tightness was intoxicating, like an ultimate barrier, and it let loose in me a wicked desire to shake you, to break you. I stretched you with both hands, my thumbs working away in your orifice as though in the middle of an unripe fruit which refuses to burst, and the other fingers tightly gripping your bum-cheeks, which leapt about in terror. I distended you, terrorised your revolt with filthy threats: I shall burst you, I shall make you crack apart, I shall burrow very deep, very deep into you, I shall bury myself in your filth and write obscene graffiti all over your body with the spoils I bring forth from you . . . I shall unveil you, uncover you, explore your entrails, I shall humiliate you, you spunk-spitting man, so proud of your virility, so strong in all your powers; we shall both come to realise that, all things considered, you're nothing more that a shit factory . . .! I shall reduce you to a state of childhood, to old age, infirmity, incontinence . . . I am opening you so wide that you won't be able to keep anything in; you can't hold yourself tight any more; you can't close yourself on your most intimate secrets . . . You have no choice: you have to share with me

40

what you have been taught to keep for yourself alone; and I'm even ahead of you – my fingers can feel things of which you are as yet unaware – unworthy things, very soft and very warm; the disturbing residues from your most hidden alchemy . . .

I stopped speaking only to go and check – whilst my hands were still pulling you apart – what I already knew: the pain had not made your erection go down. On the contrary. With my lips, I touch your enormous glans which is leaping about like a madman, very smooth, viscous, burning, stretched fit to split, divided by a deep, sharply delineated crevasse, which is also palpitating. Ah! So it excites you to have your arsehole pulled apart by someone, does it, you disgusting man? You can cry out and wriggle, but you're a queer through and through, you know. So tell me, do you like that? Do you like what my fingers are doing, do you like feeling yourself pulled apart like that? At this moment you belong to me as you have never belonged before. My fingers become completely deranged; they are going to tear you apart. And you, you are roaring and leaping up, but the cords hold good and you are still getting a bigger and bigger hard-on. What is happening to you? So, you didn't know how good it was to have something stuck up your ringpiece, eh? And believe me, there's better to come . . . Yes, tremble! Tremble good and strong, roar out loud and hope! I've brought you something really nice, and with that I'm going to send you a long, long way away. Look: do you see? It's a prick, exactly like the one I can feel at the base of my belly at this moment, very big, with a hard, swollen head, a perfect imitation . . . Ah! It's true that you can't see it – it's too dark. You can't touch it either, because you're tied up . . . I shall place it on your cheek, on your mouth, on your thighs. Have you got the measure of it? Can you imagine it? It's the biggest model I could find, and my fingers won't go round it – you'll reach heaven with that! Give me your arsehole! Give it to me, don't twist and turn, don't clench your arse – I shall stab you with it if you won't cooperate. I command you to open yourself; I command you to dilate your arse and suck it in!

41

Oh come on, open your arse and let me put it in, let me fuck you, for God's sake – you'll understand what it means to get your rocks off! Relax, more, more, push onto the glans, more, swallow it down . . . Help me, or I'll make holes in you with it! Can you feel it? It's going in . . . I feel as if it's my own prick penetrating you. Ah! That's so good! Open up, give yourself, be a female, be a whore, make a way for me, I want you, I want to bury myself in you, to lose myself in your arse, very far away, in your belly, where your heart beats, and where you distil your unclean, fascinating detritus. Give me all of you, your moistness, your odour, your tightness, your modesty. Above all your modesty. I'm coming in, make room for me. No! Don't push me out, even if it hurts a lot . . . I want it to hurt you, I want you to have atrocious colic and a terrible need to relieve yourself, I want you to be tortured by an abominable desire to shit, and, when the pressure is at its height, I shall wank your cock, and I don't know if you will climax or die . . .

I am right back inside you, I am a victorious male who is dominating you and possessing you deep down, I am your pimp, your fancy man, and you've got my fat, enormous shaft in your arse, and you're helpless. Feel me, make the most of it, you're the queer with the biggest hard-on in the world and I have only lived for this day so that I could bugger you. Now that you have swallowed it, I am going to grab hold of your big shaft and shake it, slide it up and down until you let go of everything . . . No, I can't take the prick out of your arse, even if you beg me, because I have stuffed it in completely. I'm not holding it any more. It has disappeared into your backside, and if you want to get rid of it you'll have to do it all by yourself, you'll have to push it out of you . . . And that won't be easy, because it is specially shaped to go in one way, and not to come out the other . . . Do the best you can, it's no longer my concern, I'm only trying to wank this enormous, juicy, apoplectic shaft. Push whilst I'm wanking you, push it out of you, shit it all by yourself, there's something desperate, atrocious and sublime about your efforts. You will ejaculate as you shit an enormous plastic dildo, and I will switch on the light, because, merely by watching it appear between your buttocks, I feel myself fainting with pleasure, and because I want to add to your calvary the torture of being seen like this, in the midst of your shame, torn apart between pleasure and suffering, torn asunder by the cords which you agreed to, by a strangely obscene birth, by a creature who is half man, half woman, who's beating your meat frenziedly and savouring her revenge, torn between your pleasure as a man, which is spurting out in great jets, and your pleasure as an animal, at last delivered in blood and shit . . .

Did you understand, that time, from my docile cruelty and shameless demands, how much I was depending on you?

6

You had promised that, when we next met, you would bring me a really nice surprise. I waited impatiently and also a little apprehensively for you, for I knew your character: you were a great lover of the unforeseen, the fantastic, the strange, the entirely new . . .

When you arrived, there was something bulky bulging out of your jacket pocket. The gift seemed to have no definite form, with no sharp edges; and it was a little soft and – my word – it was moving, as well. For I saw it moving slightly beneath the material before you displayed it triumphantly: it was a little cat, an adorable little grey and white pussy, with a pink nose and a fluffy coat. It began to sniff me delightfully all over, and buried its snout in my hair and in my ear, when I held it against my shoulder. My feelings were divided between tenderness and curiosity: this offering undoubtedly concealed some ulterior motive . . .

When you had undressed me with the patience and care which were so typical of you (you have to understand that my clothes lay in a disordered heap, all inside out, scattered with a tranquil immodesty all over my bedroom floor), you took hold of my shoulders and pushed me impetuously across the bed. I let myself fall and lay there with my legs hanging down and my upper body abandoned to you, knowing from experience how useless it is to resist you when you have made up your mind about a situation . . .

With a firm hand you picked up the kitten, which was wandering about all over the bedclothes, and with the other, no less firm, you pulled apart my knees. I was very obedient, opening myself up, and I heard you say: 'Now you'll see what it knows how to do!'

I had almost guessed, but when I saw you take a little carton of cream out of your other pocket, I felt myself overcome by a terrible confusion. 'No! Not that! Please, not that!'

'But of *course* that!' you replied, without the slightest awkwardness, then you bit into the corner of the carton, and tore it off with a single bite of your skilful canines. How cold that cream was in my warm, warm crack! Cold, but gentle, and as it flowed slowly (it was special 'Fleurette' brand Chantilly cream, for which I had many times found more honourable uses!), very slowly at the base of my belly, it made me shiver long and deliciously − a shiver which had very little to do with greediness, or was it perhaps to do with a very special type of greediness?

The little beast, which you were holding up by the scruff of its neck, and which you placed on my thighs, did not mew for long. Its unfailing sense of smell directed it towards me, and suddenly it began to lick me with little strokes of its minuscule rough tongue. The sensation was divinely new . . . To begin with, it attacked my pubic hair, where the cream had first fallen. It washed me conscientiously, and I felt I was being born at its caress, being brought into the world, square millimetre by square millimetre, hair by hair . . . I felt myself tormented very delicately, with great regularity, and each little bit of my skin which was attended to in this way began to vibrate under the touch.

When my pubis was decently cleansed and there wasn't the smallest drop left to lick up, the little animal pushed its nose further down between my thighs. I held my breath, feeling the animal's breathing, which was light and so disturbing, and scarcely touched my flesh with air which was a little cooler, a little warmer, I no longer knew. As always,

I was not slow in feeling incandescent in that place. The imperturbable kitten was still prospecting, with little lapping movements at the limit of what was bearable. It had just got into the most tender area between my legs, the bit where I look as if I'm starting to split in two, and it was now on my clitoris. It was enough to make anyone howl with pleasure. To give it more space and more freedom of movement, I lifted my feet, which were still on the ground, and placed them flat on the bed. Before me, you were enjoying a voyeur's delight. Your eyes were shining and you looked curiously as if you were on the lookout for something, but what did I care? I was having the nicest, most charming, most effective, most worthily named bit of pussy-licking I'd ever had.

This delicious Greymalkin's silky fur was irritating the inside of my thighs, with its lips and soft moustache it was exciting me all over, but it was above all its miraculous little tongue which was driving me wild. It wriggled down deep, brushed across my button, seized it, enveloped it, abandoned it to explore further into my furrow and then returned to it once again . . . I felt as if I were growing an unusually long clitty, stiffer and more excited than ever. I twisted about a bit, but all the same I tried to keep control of myself; on no account did I want to frighten off this sweet little animal which was so innocently sending me off to touch the skies. When it began to lick my cunt, I could have cried out with pleasure. My whole being was concentrated in the extreme: I was no longer anything more than a cunt, gaping open, sopping wet, very much alive, and throbbing with ecstasy at the touch of an eager feline mouth, whose lapping tongue made little splashing noises which resounded in such an erotic way . . .

No, really, you are always getting these ideas! I think that my shudders were a very eloquent expression of my gratitude and my admiration, and when you flooded me with a new tide of cream because the kitten seemed to have exhausted the source, this time I hollowed myself out so as to collect it more deeply within me. I should have liked it to penetrate me completely, for it to flow down into all my folds, drowning my cunt and my arse, and for that charming, madly gentle creature to come and soak me right up inside my belly . . .

With utmost docility, it began its rounds again. The thorough toilet which it was making me undergo tormented my nerves beyond imaginable limits. It mingled its fur with mine, its lips with my lips, its tongue with my button, and I no longer knew where it finished and I began, and from now on my imagination was so delirious that it invented the coupling of two fantastic beasts, with electric hair and demented movements. My pussy was making love, fucking immodestly with a neighbourhood tomcat, a dirty gutter-urchin whom I vaguely wanted to be a little repugnant, a little vulgar, a little dirty, a little brutal . . . My pussy leapt up, free from my consent, and opened itself shamelessly to call the male . . . For two pins, I would have caterwauled . . .

The grey and white kitten's coaxing, though it had brought me to fever pitch, suddenly seemed too delicate to me. I had a fiendish need, suddenly, for a bit of rough handling. I only had to call out to you and you fell upon me with your hands and your mouth. The little beast was sent packing without further ado, and you took it upon yourself to carry on its good works, with – let's admit it – a great deal more authority.

You began by grabbing handfuls of my fleece and opening me like that, without any niceties. You pulled fistfuls of my pubic hair up towards my navel, and I felt my entire cunt moving upwards, my cunt stretching vertically and my cleft getting longer. Then you pulled again on either side of the furrow, separating me like the halves of one fig which two people want to share, and I found myself offered to the maximum extent, with my cunt yawning wide fit to split, and the lips distended. Then you pulled me towards you, still holding on to my vegetation, and I felt as though my cunt was breathing, swelling up with air, and that the clitoris was no longer protected, but it was threatened by a tempest, and – curiously – that made it even stiffer . . .

When you had finished mauling me and tormenting my thatch, you placed your lips on me, and began to drink me in long, greedy, slightly cruel draughts. You bit me lightly

47

but keenly, and terror and pleasure battled within me. And he was there – the tomcat I had desired, the wild beast without scruples or delicacy, sniffing the female, biting her, making her bleed . . . You incisors played with my clitoris which, potentially suicidal, unhooded, erect and soaking wet, danced unconsciously on the keen wire of your teeth, and defied them madly. I had a terrible desire for you to lick me out, suck me off, eat me, feed from me. I should have liked to give off all the strong odours of a female in heat; I should have liked you to find the scents of musk, fish, ammonia and earth in my undergrowth and my muff. I should have liked to be the vixen, trembling underneath the fox, the wild sow forced by a harsh, powerful and hideous boar, the nanny goat mingling her wild roars with those of the he-goat. I envied the cow, thrusting her broad, dirty rump out to the bull's tongue, and the mad bitch licked voluptuously, insistently, immodestly by a loverlorn mongrel. And to think that I had often worried: Am I clean enough? Do I smell good, or at least, do I not smell too much like a woman? And here I was getting excited at the thought that the mad desire which tormented me and the juice which I could not hold back smelt strongly of love, the sea, the marshes . . . When human beings make love, they become the primitive creatures they once were, sea-wrack and mollusc, indeterminate fish; and their intimate odours, at those moments, recall very ancient times when tritons and sirens perhaps lived . . .

What did I taste like that evening? Was I salty enough, fruity enough, wild enough, spicy enough for your taste? Was I juicy enough for your greedy lips which I felt sucking at me knowingly, methodically, firmly? What effect did it have upon you to eat me after a little cat, and to feel me tremble and ripen at the touch of your mouth, and to hear me moan? Did that elate you as much as it does me when I suck your cock? Did you want, as I did in moments like that, to become a genius, a devil, to bring forth a magical pleasure, an uncontrollable delirium?

I pushed forward to meet your tongue. It was so madly persuasive, so mobile, so animal. I met your so possessive

48

lips, and I abandoned myself little by little to that famous delirium which is reminiscent of sickness, fever, dreams and visions . . . I was indeed a visionary, and an invalid too – sick with pleasure which is well given and well received, and orchestrated in a masterly way.

'My love, lick my cunt, swallow me down . . . Suck my clit like a sweetie, eat me, I'm an apricot in your mouth, a warm, warm apricot, split down the middle. And a sweet honey is running out of it. I am an overripe fig and I am bursting; no, I am transforming, and becoming a big, living shellfish – listen to the sea in my shell, eat my mussel whole, and its foam too . . . No, I'm a bitch, a bitch in heat, and my heavy-scented madness has attracted all the pooches in the district, and you are the strongest and the most disgusting of the pack, and you're sniffing me frantically, and you're licking my arse before mounting me, and when you jump me, I can feel your teeth in my neck, your clawed feet on my flanks, feel you jumping against my arse. You will seek me out, and then your dog's prick will find the way in, and you will fuck me for a long time, and I will stretch my spine and open up my arse under your stiff prick, and we shall remain stuck together, you and I, for eternity, in a very hot, very savage, heavy-scented, moist embrace: delectable . . .'

Imagining us both on all fours, one inside the other, voluptuously filthy and obscene, not caring a jot for human things and entirely given over to the fever of rutting, I burst forth under your tongue in a powerful orgasm which owed more than a little to zoological inspirations.

It really was a good idea to get that little cat.

7

The other day (quite by chance, as I believe it is a long time since he left the area), I saw charming Monsieur J. again. Yes, of course you remember him! You can't have forgotten him, because it was with him that we gave the memorable finish to a farewell evening the day before the summer holidays a couple of years ago! Don't you remember anything about it?

I was crossing a very busy avenue in Lyon. It was during the rush hour, and my attention was caught by the silhouette of someone lost in the crowd, but about six inches taller than anyone else. This man's graceful gait, which made him look almost as though he were dancing, seemed not to be at all hindered by the throng, which seemed to part miraculously to let him through. I almost cried out, shouted to him, ran to him and said: 'Do you recognise me? How's things? What have you been up to?' And then I changed my mind, preferring to let him walk away with those great elastic strides, and keep the pleasant memory he left us with that evening: to keep it for me and for you, without spoiling it with too recent news, too down-to-earth news . . .

It was late June, a warm day, and we were under the illusion that we were free, for the space of one great, extraordinary night, one night of celebration, wine and friendship.

Afterwards, all the guests went off in their respective directions, and we had that evening at our disposal to try and anaesthetise the melancholy of separation, which happened every year but was still poignant each time. I was vaguely hoping that we would be together when the dawn broke – together, you and I, for the last time for many long weeks. Mind you, this didn't prevent me from taking a full part in the joys of the drink which was duly shared.

We ate a little, danced and laughed a lot, and drank enormously.

Just before dawn, we had to get organised and leave, and that was no easy task . . . What with those who had already deserted the celebration, and those who were no longer in any fit state to do it for themselves, the number of available drivers and vehicles was more than critical. In the end, we both got into the back of some car or other, because you had just lent yours to someone – I don't know who it was, and I don't think you did either.

J. in turn asked for a lift with us, as he had just realised that he had lost his keys, and of course his car was locked. He would have to go home and find his spare set. Although the adventure wasn't exactly an exciting one, it had us in fits of laughter . . .

Our driver, who was also tolerably pissed, as he owed it to himself to be, set off with a bit of a jolt, and almost made a beautiful job of missing his first turning, as he turned the wheel using only one hand (the other one was rummaging shamelessly up his girlfriend's skirt). The car of course lurched, and I was thrown against J., who very kindly lessened the shock by putting his arm round my waist. The moment was not unpleasant. The contact of his body gave me a feeling of gentleness and safety which I rather wanted to give way to. I felt thin and small in his big encircling arm, and rather confused and troubled. But I think I owed my confusion also to a sickness of conscience, which – through the mists of the alcohol – was trying to force its way back into my memory.

I shall make the best job I can of analysing my discomfiture:

my piteous position, leaning against J.'s shoulder, ran the risk of annoying you, causing you pain, making you jealous, and on no account did I want to spoil such a delicious escapade. And so I resolved, at whatever cost, to resist his embrace and I sat forward so that he would understand and remove his arm. It was then that, taking advantage of the freedom which my movement had given you, you also slipped your arm around me, whilst of course J. didn't remove his, either. And so I found myself with two arms around me, doubly protected, settled in the narrow space between you two, whilst your two arms, about my waist, seemed to understand each other very well. It had happened so easily, so naturally, and it seemed so much agreed, so planned, so inevitable that I decided to stop asking questions . . .

The two of you both bent over me and your miraculously synchronised mouths nuzzled my neck, the hollow of my shoulder, underneath my ears, in the spot where the moistness and feverishness of a night of celebration had dampened my hair a little. You both smelled good – each of you was different, but our scents, like your caresses, like your bodies complemented each other admirably.

I then knew that the hour of my consecration had come, that the still blue-tinged dawn would see my arrival, my triumph, that I should expect to be honoured, adored and celebrated beyond my wildest dreams and fantasies . . .

All I needed to do was be a woman, a consenting woman. From then on, I was no more than a long, delicious acquiescence, from my docile neck, bending forward and shivering under your kisses, to, later on . . .

But I don't want to race by, I want to enjoy every moment, and I want you to enjoy it with me, every tiny detail of that long celebration which made me the goddess of your cult . . .

The road was winding, and each bend pressed me sometimes against him, sometimes against you. Thrown from one to the other, I sampled your differences, and grew intoxicated on your common points. An unspoken contract had been drawn up between us, granting me dispensation from every hypocritical form of protest. I didn't have to say no, and in any case, if I had done it would hardly have sounded convincing; I didn't even have to pretend I was slightly indignant, or ask myself questions, or think about anything at all.

Your hands began to be rivals, competing to see which could be bolder in touching me, and I let them have full freedom, aiding their task from time to time. Very quietly, I rejoiced that I was so completely binary, and suddenly I was even surprised that a single man could have been enough for me up to now. I was wearing a very light bustier, with obliging straps which you had suddenly known how to get on to your side: you took hold of one strap each, and slid them down off my shoulders; one shoulder each to caress, to stroke, and whose roundness and softness you emphasised, each on his own side.

Then the bustier gave way, and my breasts came into view. One breast each. The share-out was arranged in advance, and your hands which had already touched them through the silk bodice, took hold of them with a warm authority. I didn't know to which side my heart inclined, on which side I was better caressed, better cared for, better aroused. Both of my nipples were equally erect, and I felt as if I were being stroked, kneaded, fondled by two Siamese twins with perfectly simultaneous gestures, or even by a single man and his reflection, in a mirror positioned exactly in the middle of me. This harmony of gestures and sensations was maintained perfectly: was it possible that two men could carry out the same action in the same second?

I abandoned myself to your caressing, touching, slightly breathless from the pleasure which was taking me over, my bosom swollen and trembling beneath your fingers. It's better on the left! No, the right! No, everywhere! Oh! I don't know which breast I should devote myself to, and I wait, without being disappointed, for your two mouths to settle upon me at the same time, and drink me in long draughts . . . If I have any more children, I want only twins, I've decided. One on each teat – it's so good it almost makes me come . . .

And then your hands flew off together like a couple of turtle doves, and settled on my knees: one knee each, and one thigh each, climbing up, exploring, sculpting me. Without taking account of the two other occupants of the car, I began to moan with pleasure, and perhaps also with anguish. Confusedly, I felt the fatal moment approaching when your hands would follow the contours of the treasures of my symmetry, when they would arrive together at the single frontier which divided me . . . What would then happen? Would I become a land to conquer by force, or maybe a no-man's-land respected by both of you? No, no, not a no-man's-land, no respect, no neutrality, you have warmed me up, aroused me, excited me too much, and you must come to some arrangement to establish a satisfactory treaty. I was counting on you enormously to sort yourselves out or even fight, but above all, above all, no no-man's-land and no retreating from the field of battle!

But my anxiety was still premature. You were in no hurry and you wandered all over me with diabolical grace and a similarity of gestures which was making me mad. There was no trace in you of that sporting rivalry which drives the alpine climber to plant his flag before his opponent. As regards the flag, each of you possessed a flagpole of fine dimensions, which I discovered at the same time on my right and my left, with a hand – with two hands – which were eager and astonished. What? The same sorcery there, too? The same equality? I was Alice in Wonderland, and I was living at the same time on both sides of the mirror, touching the same two men here and there, two men with the same postures, the same preoccupations, the same bodies, the same pricks . . .

In my hands I could feel two swellings of equal size, a rigidity of equal dynamism. Caressing two phalluses at the same time doubled my confusion, not to mention my moans and my rather lewd dance. I was calling two men to me, with the mad desire that they would come together and that the enchantment would last to the end, to both ends . . .

You had reached the softest, most velvety, tenderest parts of me: that intimate place where the thigh is no longer quite part of the leg, and it is not yet the cunt. You wandered about for a long time, running the tips of your fingers over that privileged by not very spacious area, without ever meeting (I was very cooperative, and spread my legs with a rare good will), and what's more, without either of you setting off on a bolder path.

So much did I hope you would go higher, waiting for you and fearing, that little by little I lost my footing, and my panting made the passenger in the front seat turn round. She caught us in mid-debauchery, but her rather incredulous look did not make me close either my eyes or my legs.

And yet, little by little, you slipped under the hem of my knickers, still perfectly, irresistibly together. I felt you invading me gently, first reaching the hip joint, then my pubic hair, then the outer lips of my cunt. This slow, demoniacal progression made my heart thump wildly. I desired, I was in a hurry, I was hot, I was afraid . . . I no longer really knew what I had, since I did not have you, and my impatient fingers still feeling your hard, hard shafts swelling in your pants.

The better to caress me and excite me, and also to respect the unspoken agreement of absolute joint ownership, you both made the same movement at the same second, dictated by the same impulse: you rolled the edges of my panties into my cleft, thus reducing my gusset to a thin roll of crumpled fabric which from now on provided the real frontier between my right-hand lover and my left-hand lover. It was horribly arousing: the material ran right against my clitoris, which began to rub itself against it energetically, and on my vagina, which had already been growing wet for some time and was almost throbbing in time with my heart. Everything which lay beyond this limit on one side or the other was subject to your tortures, your irritations, your games.

Pleasure and desire made me lift my buttocks off the seat, and move about all over the place. I was almost on the point of begging in a loud voice for a truce or a more decisive offensive when the car stopped. We were outside J.'s apartment block. As naturally as you please, he suggested: 'Come in and have a drink. We can sort the keys out later.'

As naturally as you please, our driver and his companion refused. As naturally as you please, you and I accepted.

J.'s door was next to the pavement. He opened it, and got out. I was afraid that you might open the other door, and get out on the other side, for I would then be faced with the symbolic obligation to choose one way rather than the other. But, with great intuition, you waited for me to follow J. and then followed me . . .

We three all got out into the street, and the others drove off. And then you took my left arm and he took my right – an arm each – and our trio went off happily towards the door to the building. I wasn't really touching the ground, seeing as I was hooked on to you two, who were taller than I was, and overcome by the double intoxication of what I had drunk during the evening, and lived through in the car . . .

As we reached a bend in the passageway, a vast mirror sent back an image of a woman with ruffled hair, a little dishevelled and solidly surrounded by two gallants with a gleam in their eyes.

In the lift, for a moment, I rediscovered all the night's emotions, which had seen me dancing cheek-to-cheek with more than one dancer. Slowly, and over a long period of time, I had developed against the bodies of men who were all different, all charming, in an atmosphere of suggestive warmth, enveloping arms and an erotic rhythm. Several times my belly had felt the burgeoning excitement of my partner of the moment, and had in turn been excited by it. And now here I was, in this smooth, carpeted lift cabin, feeling the same dizziness taking me over again, but this time it was much more voluptuous because you were both there to embrace me. You held me against you, but with my back towards you, offering me courteously to the other man, who accepted the invitation and pressed up against my bosom and my belly firmly. I felt you were both tense, hurried, alive and feverish. Your hands ran over my body, and so did your mouths, all over my hair, my neck, everywhere, and I abandoned myself to a delicious astonishment: the astonishment of finding myself in the midst of you, the astonishment of being the crossroads of your desires, and of touching you so perfectly, so together, so well with the two sides of my body. I became a double entity: my shivering, enchanted back belonged to you, arched and with my buttocks thrusting out, rubbing against your prick, but my breasts belonged to him and he was crushing them; and so did my belly and my pubis, where he too was imprinting the fierce bas-relief of his virility . . .

My wide, light skirt, which had allowed you so many liberties in the car, did not hinder you now, either: you began to lift it up and together, your hands took hold of my thighs, my legs . . .

You both fell to your knees almost at the smae time. The lift had stopped at the floor we had selected, but no one had noticed. I was leaning back against the carpeted wall, so as not to give way to the giddiness which was overwhelming me; I spread my legs a little, feet firmly planted in their high heels, and closed my eyes. Your fingers began once again to finger me terrifyingly between my skin and my knickers, which earlier caresses had already made soaking wet.

The discomfort of the situation, its precariousness, and this tortured wait which you were inflicting on me, became unbearable. The desire to be fucked was so torturing me that I bent my knees, closed my eyes, moaned and raved . . .

He was first to get up and open his door for us. We followed him into his flat, not noticing anything about the decor except a very low sofa which I collapsed on to, calling to you with my hospitable legs and arms, my heart turned upside down, and my modesty in full flight.

You didn't get undressed. You just unbuttoned your flies . . . I thought I was seeing double, when you knelt before me and showed me 'them'. A man's prick, nice and erect, proud, aroused, has an hallucinatory quality when you have fire in your arse and a sopping wet cunt, but two of them! The night was taking on all the trappings of a sabbath, a black mass – and I was to be the victim, promised to a delicious sacrifice.

When you turned me over, I didn't put up any resistance.

Nor when you took off my knickers. My arms and torso were on the sofa, my knees on the ground and my head somewhere in the stars. My skirt, which a skilful hand (whose was it?) had just unfastened, had slipped from my waist and I don't think anyone bothered to pick it up. It lay there on the ground, around me, a mere rag which was now useless and hindered us not a bit. I stuck out my backside towards you, and I guessed that you were no longer caressing me with your hands. You had allowed your madly gentle, hard, burning pricks to stray all over me, and I concentrated so as to sense as completely as possible every delicate, velvety, elastic movement they made. At one point, one of them worked its way in a little further, settled on my arsehole, and I felt it become a little sticky and so persuasive . . . If it had wanted, I would have swallowed it up, very greedily, but it withdrew to return again (was it the same one or the other?) and made me even wetter. I had two entrances for you, equally welcoming, one dripping all on its own, and the other which you were lubricating intelligently, with your own juices . . . I was waiting, hoping, calling out to couple with you, whilst seeking another word rather than 'couple', because that implies two and there were three of us. I didn't want to move, or impose, or choose.

One of you said (at that moment I could no longer recognise your voices): 'Do you want us?'

Very quickly I replied: 'Yes!'

'Both of us?'

'Yes!'

'How?'

'Everywhere!'

Who was it who put his arm round my waist and lifted me up? Who sat down where I had been sitting on the seat which was so obligingly low? I don't remember any more. All I can visualise is his clothes in disarray, and that obscene, oversized prick, tempting enough to make you howl as it emerged from his trousers. I didn't think and I accepted the proposition. I got astride him, and swallowed him up very quickly. His shaft slid into me as though by remote control, all on its own and at top speed. Behind me, the other one (which one was it?) worked its way in. He placed his hands on my waist, and the head of his knob methodically began its search. When it felt itself on the threshold it pushed lightly, and I came out to meet it, opening myself to savour its penetration, millimetre by millimetre. The pad which rubbed against it as it passed in made me give a moan of painful ecstasy, and then it was deep inside me, and moved no more.

Taken in front and from behind at the same time, stuffed with two equally stiff shafts, I began a strange kind of voyage, full of marvels, incredulous, almost mystical. From the first step, I raised myself up slowly, very slowly, so as not to lose either of you, and then fell back, just as slowly. With my gentleness and earnest efforts, I tamed your two wild pricks. I made room for them; and they must have felt so close together, recognising each other; and when they bumped against each other it sent a demented shiver through me . . . Then I set the rhythm, and you waited, unmoving, and allowed me to pump away at you with an admirable concentration and stoicism.

I felt as though I were being stuffed to bursting, as though this invasion must make me explode, and yet I moved on you, I danced, I became light and took wing, and my entire body took part in the celebration. I was sucking you with my two mouths, eagerly, with the feeling that I had wanted and needed to do so for so long, so long, that nothing could perhaps fulfil this delay of our orgasms. I absorbed you seriously, with passion, and I only allowed you to emerge from me the better to take you inside me again, more deeply, further inside. I wanted you to be even longer, fatter, more turgid; I wanted to stimulate you for as long as you had excited me, and I knew that simple politeness and the niceness which you shared would forbid you from abandoning yourselves to pleasure before me. Oh! How well you have been brought up! I heard your breathing grow wilder and tried to control mine as much as I could. I even came down to earth a little, because I was dreaming of making this double embrace last beyond the possible, because its daring perfection might never be found again.

One of you, very close to capitulation, whispered very quickly and very low: 'Wait, wait, stop moving!'

I stopped, because there was something pleading and urgent about his voice.

All three of us remained still for a few minutes, but I could not manage to control the throbbing of my cunt. Inside me it was sucking away and I could do nothing about it. I pictured myself as a sort of boa constrictor with a monstrous double mouth, swallowing down a two-headed, voluminous, vibrant prey . . . I knew I mustn't dwell too long on what was happening between my thighs, between my buttocks, because I would soon have lost all control of my body . . . I must not think about your pricks, all warmed up, sheathed and tightly ringed by my most secret flesh. I must not picture them, imperious, engorged with sap, sticky, foaming, strangled in my pulsating flesh. I resisted, resisted pleasure very hard although it was radiating through me, dilating me, making me burst . . .

It was you who said: 'Stroke yourself!', as though you were saying 'Hurry up and come, I can't bear it any longer!', and I refused to comply, knowing that my skilful finger, should it touch my clitoris for a second, would immediately ignite the gunpowder.

And so you both sought me out yourselves, and it was diabolical to feel myself being taken, pinched, kneaded, tortured all over at once. You composed a string quartet on me, playing with my breasts, my hips, my buttocks and my cunt with the enthusiasm of virtuoso performers. And you invented magical words to this infernal, enchanting symphony, incantations which hypnotised me and took away all my will. It was difficult for you to move together without the risk of breaking our fragile balance. But your words alone turned me on, more effectively than if you had both been able to wank me off as you pleased.

I felt myself still clenched around your two pricks which were throbbing away equally, and I heard your murmurs, your prayers, your words which wore down my resistance little by little. You said to me: 'Come!' and 'Let go!', you urged me: 'Go on, climax! Enjoy us! Swallow us up, let it come, let yourself go, talk, cry out, sing, howl a little, and we'll accompany you!' You asked me: 'Can you feel us? Are you enjoying fucking us? Are we big enough for you? Are we filling you right up? What do you think of us?' You commented: 'You're moving, you're breathing, you're sucking us in, you're making us grow, you have a burning cunt, a flaming arse, you're going to make us burst, you're a good fuck, you're dripping wet, even your arsehole is getting wet . . .' You demanded, 'Come on, wank yourself off! Get on with it! Make us come with you! Come on, gallop!' You warned me: 'We aren't going to stay like this for long, we're going to let go, and send all our spunk up into your cunt and your arse, you little whore who refuses to come!'

And in spite of your orders, your threats, your vulgar remarks and your insults, you were still so nice, so courteous, so submissive that I ended up giving in, placing my finger on the button which you had both tried in vain to switch on (I'm the only one who knows the secret), and in the end I started moving rhythmically up and down on your fevered shafts again, sat down on you so you went right up inside me and I was well and truly impaled, buggered, really enjoying taking you and letting you go, polishing you, smoothing you, wanking you, concentrating on the countdown which had just begun . . . One minute and counting! I have an electric cunt and I'm hot all over, all over . . . Forty seconds, and I'm not letting you go any more, I'm not losing you, you belong to me forever . . . Twenty seconds, and it's going to burst out all over the place, everywhere, all my orifices are opening, I have terrible desires . . Ten seconds, and I want to shit, piss, run, run away, stay, howl . . . Five seconds . . . to die . . . Three contracted, tense, erect, torn apart . . . Two, then one, the desire and need to shout out 'I love you!' with I don't know which mouth, since I no longer exist, all I am now is an immense cunt which has just exploded . . .

I gave myself up to pleasure with all my being, all my consciousness, with the very depths of me. The orgasm completely submerged me, transported me, overcame me. Its waves washed through me again and again for a long time with the same force, and when I felt your pricks softening, I came again because of them, my fingers, your sighs, my cries, I came again and I trembled, vibrated, arching my back the better to keep you inside me . . .

Had we reached the same port exactly together, had we come alongside at the same second? I didn't know, but I retained an ecstatic memory of the voyage, a precious, delectable stiffness, a delicious burning whose waves were still shaking me with a convulsion related to the sob of a little child, the fever of a sick animal.

I spent my convalescence on the carpet, flat on my belly and with my head buried in my folded arms, listening to the tumultuous sounds of joy gradually diminishing. I had left you, abandoned both of you, not knowing which of you I ought to snuggle against with what remained to me of my ardour and pleasure.

But you had rejoined me, and were now lying beside me (one on either side, do I really need to mention that now?), and yet without quite touching me. The heat which radiated from your bodies sank gently into me and I lost myself in a nameless sense of wellbeing, a blessed torpor over which two solicitous guardians might be watching . . .

After a little while, I lifted my head, looked at you and noticed that you still had not undressed . . . I decided, vaguely, that I would undress you, but allowing myself a few seconds more respite, and at the moment of choosing which of you I was going to start on first, I fell asleep . . .

You must undoubtedly have caressed me during this unexpected truce. Through the thickness of my sleep, I felt waves of warmth running through me. I felt as though I were floating in a warm bath, or burrowing into a soft pillow, and the warmth and softness soaked right through me. I began to dream. It was a strange dream, sumptuous and obscene. I was in the arms of a very tall, very fat woman, with enormous breasts, and she was rubbing herself against me. Her bosoms were swaying against me very gently and completely, first against my face, which I had buried in her chest, and then my own breasts, and then – for she had knelt down – my belly, my cunt, my thighs. She turned me round, then moved back up me, still using her two fat cushions of flesh to follow the swell of my calves, the line of my buttocks, into which she pressed them. I parted my legs to feel the softness of her breasts on the inside surface of my thighs and in the opening of my crack. I began to desire her madly; I would have liked her to make love to me with her chest as her tits became more and more persuasive. She knew how to run her nipples over mine with an audacious hand, and this delicious rubbing sent electric shocks running through me . . .

She said: 'Look how erect I am!' and it was true. Her nipples had lengthened; the teats had grown and hardened, and you'd have said they were two fingers, pointing at me. I was astounded, anguished, confused. She forced me to lie down on the ground, knelt down, pulled my legs towards her, laid my buttocks upon her imposing thighs, and pulled me open. 'Open wide your cunt,' she told me, 'I want to give you one . . .' And she did! First, I felt the long, hard nipple pressing against my cunt and sliding inside, and then I opened myself, opened wide, and her breast slid into me, right up to its base. The feeling of being torn apart was more pleasurable than painful to me. I was taken over by it, overwhelmed, filled to overflowing.

'Come on, suckle me!' she ordered. 'Like when you were little. You liked that, didn't you, sucking at mummy's titties? Go on, drink, you're a tiny child!' And so I drank. I had a real mouth between my thighs, and I sucked her with it. She was running with a very thick liquid, and I wasn't even surprised by this miracle until I noticed the taste. It was sweetish, sugary, and the tide submerged me, drowned my cunt, overflowed into my cleft and ran down to my arse. I was covered in the stuff, and I would have liked to be washed and dried, but the milk kept on flowing, and my starving cunt kept on sucking, sucking . . .

63

I awoke in a state of some excitement. I had turned over in my sleep and was now lying on my back; and you were stroking my belly and my pubis with a light touch. I was soaked through because my cunt was dripping with the last traces of our previous pleasure, perhaps also because my dream had aroused me greatly. I put my hand on my cunt, which a single, trickling drop was titillating, and I lingered there willingly, still under the influence of my dreamlike emotions . . .

You exchanged a long, incredulous, indignant look that said: 'No! Surely she's not going to bring herself off in front of us, now?' Oh yes I was! That was a truly amusing, charming, spicy idea . . . Showing you how I can make myself come all by myself, how I can get by without all your little tricks. Suddenly, I had the desire, after wanting you so much earlier on, to defy you a little, to vex you a little. My little nap had made me a present of a pleasure which was absolutely, uniquely feminine – where you had no place, with your big aggressive pricks, and it pleased me to make its strange, but torrid atmosphere last longer.

'Look how easy it is to forget you, my darlings, how simple it is to do without you! I am a perfectly tuned, perfectly autonomous machine. My left hand is the engine. With the thumb, I find my cunt. It's very soft, very welcoming. I find the way in, settle in, dance a little inside it. With the index finger, I penetrate my arse. Not like you, not so roughly. I don't have to force or push, I have nothing to do. I place the tip of my finger on it, lightly, as though I was knocking politely on someone's door when I knew they were expecting me, and I let things happen . . . My arse is very civilised. It knows the way to invite, to greet, to open itself. It's small, warm, tight, intimate in there. But when you have the knack, it soon gets very soft, and you can go in very deep. Look how far in I'm going with my two fingers, how well I'm holding myself, how well I'm gratifying myself! My thumb is on the loose, it's swimming in a warm swamp with throbbing banks, in a river whose bed is indeterminate, but so soft, so comfortable . . .

'My index finger is taking liberties, trying to enlarge the corridor it's moving down a little, and it's divinely good to bugger yourself like that, all alone, very nicely. I don't govern my own movements any more. My hand is very intelligent – it's the best mistress, the best lover I have ever had. Only my hand knows where it can go, where it can bury itself . . . Only it can pinch me like that, from the inside, very far between the buttocks, or the arse, I don't know which, and with two well-manoeuvred fingers feel the elasticity of this curtain which separates my two holes . . .

'The other hand is the starter motor. It has an almost infallible knack for organising voyages, carrying me far away, and high, and for a long time. But I don't put it in charge of the expedition right away; an itinerary like the one I have decided to follow requires preparation. So my right hand, which doesn't like having nothing to do, takes care of the luggage. I want to leave well prepared, well dressed, well laden with pleasure, desire, impatience . . . That's why it is so diligent, my right hand. You can see how delicately it parts my lips, as though it were carefully drawing me: the contour of the great lips, the sensitive spot where they join, above, their two completely symmetrical ravines around the petal in the middle . . . You can see how my fingers understand each other, there too, as to how to make me shiver, to make me react. They have long learned all the strategic points, and all the effects of each of their caresses: here, that opens my thighs; there, that tightens my bum-cheeks; there again, that makes me stick out my belly; if they touch me here, I pant; higher up, and I twist about; lower down, and I push right down on my left hand, which is very competent and comes out to meet me . . .

'But for a long, long time – until I give the order to touch it – the fingers of my right hand will avoid this arrogant button of flesh, in the heart of all my meanderings, this little animal which is so lively, so stubborn, so hard to tame, but so faithful when you have gained its confidence; for a long time they will stay away, despite my desire, and its desire too, for me to reach the clitoris, which must be both

65

awakened and controlled, alarmed and respected at the same time. Let it reach the point when it can take no more imposed chastity, let it surrender, let its minuscule, terrified head come of its own accord to greet the embrace, and only after then, with my exclusive permission, may my finger (always the same one) touch it, first with calm and assurance, to feel its touching dynamism, its moving ardour . . .

'After that, I won't be answerable for anything. It sparks and flames simultaneously, and they are inextinguishable. My right hand is waltzing in the flames with a speed which is confined to vibration; it's a wild, extravagant musician, a gypsy woman abandoned to the dance, swaying and swirling like a woman possessed. Look, take a good look, and look quickly, because it's not going to last: I'm fucking myself on my own and I love that, and I'm climaxing because I'm open in front of you, and obscene, and animal, and a sorceress . . . I'm climaxing because I'm imagining you, replacing you, supplanting you, and I'm even going to cry out, and twist and turn and close my eyes, and freeze at the summit of my joy, my whole body tensed, burning, filled with marvels . . .

'The journey went without a hitch, through grandiose scenery. And the objective has been reached . . .'

I come back to earth and find you still there. And that pleases me. I had rather forgotten you during my wanderings. I wanted above all to talk to you, and then, you know what it's like – you get carried away . . . Well? How have things been since I left? What's new? You've changed, you know . . . Your expressions, your faces have changed – handsome faces, by the way, with flattering contrasts. Nervous, brown curls on one side, frothy blondish waves on the other; a square jaw and energetic features here, there, a softer, dreamier, and more finely drawn physionomy; the eyes on my left hesitate between yellow and green, whilst an uncertain sky, sometimes grey and sometimes blue, tints those on my right. I find you handsome, and different, and perhaps handsome because you are different. Get undressed! How big you are, my darling, my big boy, my familiar one, and how delicately built he is, the unknown (or almost), the new man, the unexpected . . . And to think I saw you as being the same, just a little while ago!

It was inevitable that the alcohol and the night would dim my eyes. Dawn has broken completely, and I am watching you, my two dawn lovers, moving, as dissimilar as you had seemed identical to me before. Your body is more stocky, more square, more solid . . . Your virility also has its own personality, the modest blond, in spite of its excitement, because it always does its best to retain a modest demeanour, an attitude at the limit of timidity; the vehement dark man, vindictive, because you like to make an exhibition of yourself, and you voluntarily delegate ambassadorial powers to your virility.

He's a poet, an artist; and it's not until after the event that you realise, with a slight surprise, that he has a prick and knows how to use it. For you, it's the opposite: you first of all get acquainted by means of your cock, and then are astonished to discover, afterwards, and only afterwards, that it hides (and you'll allow me this flattering expression) the man.

Here you both are, naked and erect – he reservedly, you ostentatiously, and I fall in love with your duo. I would like to make ardent, unexpected declarations to you, but I haven't learned how to speak words of love in the plural . . . And so my mouth closes on tendernesses which I shall keep for myself alone, and I shall content myself with reading in your eyes the interest which I have aroused whilst I shamelessly wanked myself off in front of you.

The manoeuvre has visibly excited you. You have a terrible look of concentration, almost to the point of bewilderment, anguish. A lewd curiosity has made you bend towards me, has frozen you in an animal attitude of watching, stopping, careful, silent hunting. When I asked you to get undressed, you did so with veiled gestures, the restraint of stowaways, because neither of your wanted to spoil this state of extreme attention, which has irritated your nerves and swollen your pricks.

And now you are staring at me soundlessly, without moving . . . It's the intense pause, the eternal second before the cat pounces . . . But I'm not saying anything, either. On my skin, I can feel your gazes burning, and waves run through me, like a calm water rippled by a stormy wind . . .

Paradoxically, I suddenly understand how much I love you. You, you alone, even through him whom I desire. Do you feel the same? Are you thinking the same thing I'm thinking, at the same moment? Glance away from me for a moment, turn towards him, and look at him looking at me, look at him desiring me, looking at me in detail, appreciating me. Adore me, not as I am, but as he sees me, as other men see me whom I seduce without loving them. Can you feel how precious I am, how beautiful I am, how tempting I am for him, at this moment? Aren't you proud to possess me, more tender, more grateful, more gratified, more taken with me, aren't you in a word more jealous at the moment when you are giving me to him and when he is going to take me? And aren't you flattered too, that I should please him, more sure of my feelings for you, of my admiration, my tenderness, since you know that I am sensitive to men's charms, but proccupied only with you, my love?

The moment lasts, and I reign over your hopes, adorned in each of your eyes by the look which the other man is giving me. Your fervour is fed each by the other, and the emulation which did not exist when we arrived here has just been born out of this disturbing game of glances. Each one seems to be confessing: 'I want her even more because you want her too!' Here I am at the centre of a rivalry without animosity or spite, but not without nobility, and I am waiting for you – my lords, my masters, my slaves.

The relaxation of tension was double and, once again, perfectly simultaneous. Your joint strength lifted me up off the ground, and carried me off towards the bar which I hadn't noticed before in a corner of the living room. You were sitting on one of the tall bar stools arranged round it. Our frolics were going to take on some altitude . . .

I turned my back to you, and perched myself on the cross

bars which joined the legs of the stool. You took hold of my waist, very quickly, with both hands. Your stiffened, maddened prick was under my arse. With a firm pressure you put me on to it, and I cried out with the shock. He was there, in front of me, standing exactly at the right height, and I saw his glistening, maddened prick beating out a funny sort of rhythm. You put your hands under my thighs and lifted them up, parted them, opening me right up and I came down again on to your shaft, and you held me like that, absolutely open to the other man, whose desire was growing needle-sharp and pierced me through without further ado.

It was he who set the rhythm for us. You simply held me, and as I was wedged between the two of you, impaled on your two stakes, dripping wet and panting, I just let things happen. In front of me, he was dancing a frenzied scalping dance, or rain dance, or love dance. He didn't just grind backwards and forwards, but from left to right, enlarging me noticeably, as if he wanted to make me gape wide open. Then his movements became circular, his hips turned quickly and his prick drew perfect circles within me, and I felt as if my cunt was forming enchanted Os.

Behind me, you could feel the repercussions of his pile-driving, and you were panting into my neck. A storm was tossing me about, and I was a little afraid of capsizing, but the pleasure which was beginning to take me over soon took over from terror and pain. You had violated me a little, and the burning of your penetration was beginning to turn into a terribly suggestive warmth.

I savoured your pricks, and their sliding and their volume, before I set my sights on pleasure. He was the reason for my stoicism, with a gesture which, at that moment, I found irresistibly erotic: with his hands, which were still free, he picked up the mass of his balls and crushed them between the two of us, under his shaft and against my pubic hair, at the base of my cunt, squeezing very tight against me and murmuring wildly: 'Can you feel them? Can you feel them?' At that moment, it seemed more decent if I too lost my composure, and I wanked my little button with a frenzied eagerness as yet unequalled that night.

When I began to moan, I heard you whispering in my ear, in a rather different voice: 'So, little slut, anyone would think you loved us more. So tell me: isn't what we're giving you better than with your fingers?' I agreed, I cried out yes, yes, that it was good, very good, terrific, wonderful, and only after that capitulation did you ejaculate with trembling and spasms and moaning, gestures which I perceived as a form of homage . . .

It was broad daylight, and a beautiful day . . . We left him, then parted ourselves, and I kept the feeling that you had offered me that night a little as if it were a farewell present, an ambiguous present, which would leave me twice as much nostalgia for you, twice as much emotion, and twice as much desire to see you again. . . .

8

It began as a game. When you arrived at my place, you found me at my desk.

'Still writing?'

'You know perfectly well that I'm a paper woman,' I replied.

And then you took hold of me by the waist, in one of those affectionate, impetuous gestures so typical of you, and you hustled and manhandled me a little until at last I lay down, still protesting, on the desktop, which was laden with notes, notepads, notebooks and dictionaries . . .

'Come here, paper woman, come to your rightful place!' you commanded me and, in the end, I lay down obediently between my typewriter and the pot I kept my pencils in, on the big blotter I used as a writing pad.

Very quickly, you pulled apart the sides of my dressing gown (though 'undressing gown' would have been a better name for it, that day). Underneath it I was naked; you began by caressing me all over, rapidly, as you might smooth a white sheet of paper with the flat of your hand before writing the first words of a letter.

You sat down on my chair. It was a secretary's swivelling chair, very high and mounted on castors. I felt as though I were a patient, subjected to a doctor's examination, and this idea, which had often haunted my fantasies, excited me even more surely than your hands.

You took hold of a black felt pen, with a very thick, moist tip, and you began to execute some very strange calligraphy work on me . . . 'I am going to turn you into a dictionary of love,' you told me, and, making your actions speak as loudly as your words, you placed the pen on my neck and wrote, declaiming the words loudly as you went along: 'Neck: part of the body reserved for tender, exciting kisses.' The definition which you had noted down started underneath my right ear, went along my cleavage, and disappeared under my left ear. This necklace of words with which you had just bedecked me was only the first of a series which I hoped would be very long and increasingly suggestive.

Next, you ringed each of my arms, halfway between the shoulder and the elbow, with a bracelet of little black letters which you wrote carefully and conscientiously. 'Arm,' you wrote on the left one. 'Limb which you open in order to kiss.' And on the right: 'Arm, limb which you close when embracing.' The tip of the felt pen was titillating me deliciously, especially on the inner surface of my arms, at that spot where the skin is so fine, so well protected and so secret that it always remains whiter than anywhere else.

On, or rather in, my hands, you wrote: 'Hands: the workers of love – caressing, handling, wanking.' I abandoned myself to the nervous touch of this pentip, which was running over my open palms and, in its own way, redrawing my lifeline and my line of fortune. You also took hold of my fingers, but seemed in a little difficulty. 'So which one is it, then?' you asked, and – without saying a word – I replied with a gesture which might have been interpreted as obscene, but hadn't we already come to that, bearing in mind the direction which events were taking? And so you noted down on the middle finger of my right hand, still on the inner surface: 'Clitty finger' and, by deduction, you easily defined certain other fingers on my left hand, in a way which I found a little crude (but how am I to stop you once you get an idea in your head?), and named them 'Cunt finger' and 'Arse finger'. I

72

didn't find the fantasy unpleasant, and this pen was starting to acquire a strange power over me. But I hadn't seen anything yet!

When you moved to my breasts, I shuddered slightly. Already you were writing away, surrounding each of the two globes with scrawled concentric circles, which got smaller as they moved inwards towards the nipple. You intoned: 'Breasts: twin roundnesses of variable volume and consistency, proscenium of the theatre of amorous activities.' The contact was both exciting and painful, because with a very firm left hand you were compressing the base of my bosom, so that you could use your right hand to write on the less mobile, less elastic flesh. You had gathered the mass of my breast in your powerful fingers, and your pen was scribbling away with a firm, rather obligingly cruel, pressure.

I was still hesitating between suffering and pleasure, when you came down to my belly and covered it with rather frenzied graffiti: 'Belly: last stop before the cunt, follow the arrows,' and with big black strokes you drew lots of arrows converging towards a single, even blacker point . . .

On the inside of my thighs, you wrote: 'Thighs: to be pulled apart in order to fuck. The entrance is this way.' And I received more arrows, but these ones were pointing upwards. I was a bit worried I'd get the old 'Shake well before use', but it was too late – already you were turning me over, ripping off my one remaining garment (if you can really call the light, crumpled veil which scarcely covered me a garment)to scribble all over my back and buttocks.

There, the young kid (or the artist) in you awoke completely: I felt myself striped with long lines, and I think that, on my reverse side, I was more like a road map than any other sort of document. The itinerary which you were recommending was direct and without turn-offs. It led roughly down from the nape of my neck to my bum-cheeks, and from the apex of my buttocks it led along several possible paths, all of equal length, into my intimate valley. If you wanted to start from my legs, for example, from the back of my knees, the road to follow was quite clearly delineated:

73

a long line to the fold of my buttocks, and a smaller one (a sort of forest path) to climb back up to the meeting-point. When Stevenson wrote *Treasure Island*, he showed less fervour and less imagination than you, you who were now ringing the place to which all your meanderings led, with a cabbalistic sign in black ink: it was my arsehole, which I clenched tight as I felt your attack, for the point of your pen was making itself felt very authoritatively . . .

And then you decided to brighten up these over-dark pages which you had just blackened with a monotonous pen. 'Paper woman, I am going to make you up!' you said, and you chose a red marker pen and used it to tint the tips of my breasts, for you had just turned me over again on the desk, exactly like a rough draft which you read and reread, go over and add things to.

Next, you slid a hand roughly between my thighs and declared: 'There are some well-hidden pages in this book,' and you set out to unmask their secret, to dishonour their modesty . . . You made my whole cunt red, painting it with bold strokes of your bloody paintbrush, sparing nothing, forcing your way into the tiniest fold, scribbling with the same enthusiasm on the insides of the outer lips, drawing delicately on the inner ones, and the entrance to the vagina; when you moved across my clitoris, I could not prevent myself from crying out in pain, for your touch was so brutal . . .

The ink which you were using to make me up so vigorously soon began to burn my fragile tissues, and I tried to get up and go into the bathroom. But you held me down forcibly on the table, and decreed that the work of art was far from finished. The burning sensation I was feeling had a rather ambiguous quality to it: it felt at once as though someone had rubbed me with ice cubes, and as if a very big, very hot hand was taking possession of my intimate parts.

I then realised, from the spasms of my cunt, that a strange form of sensual pleasure was developing from this irritation. It was the first time that I had so literally felt my arse on fire.

'Blow on it, it's burning too much!' I begged.

'No, I'm going to do you in style.'

Fear made me squeeze my legs together, but you were stronger than I was and my cunt was even more painful when I closed it again.

You had just found quite a fine paintbrush, and you began to caress me with it ingeniously. Using the tips of the hairs, you were scrupulously and methodically trying to follow all the lines of a geometry which ended up vibrating with excitement. You were recreating me, you were redrawing me, like a diligent artist, and I felt myself becoming a work of art under your hand, the magnificent rose window of a waiting, expectant cathedral . . .

Your minuscule brush forgot nothing. It wriggled itself into the tiniest fold, rose and fell ten times, one after the other, along my crack, tickling my clitoris, titillating the entrance to my vagina, and it seemed to me that my cunt was opening, slowly spreading out, like a flower almost bursting to your naked eye, petal after petal. The burning of the ink had exaggerated my sensitivity, and the lascivious dance of your paintbrush soon became intolerable. Between my thighs I had a sort of monstrous water lily of living flesh, full blown, offered, burning, immodest . . .

My orifices were open, relaxed, completely tamed by your caresses, maddened with pleasure, and I could feel them pulsating, dilating to call you, contracting so that they could dilate even more. I begged you, 'Fuck me! Come, come into me . . .', but you suddenly took on a mysterious worrying air. I guessed that this was no longer the facetious little boy, the young scribbler talking in you, when you replied: 'You don't fuck a paper woman with a prick . . .'

What evil genie inspired you then? What devil was driving you? I saw a wicked gleam flash through your eyes, and at the same moment both of us thought of that genial, deranged marquis, divine and satanic, who marked literature with his savage, refined imagination and his hallucinatory fantasies . . .

If I had really wanted, I could have run away and refused your demands, but a perverse curiosity kept me at the table, as did a bizarre desire: I wanted to know just how far you could go, and I with you, how far the love of the torturer for his victim and of the victim for her torturer can go. With you, I wanted to triumph over boring daily life and taboos, I wanted to offer you my submission like an extraordinary jewel, and damn myself with you rather than give up . . . I wanted to become your creature, I wanted to become your Justine . . .

You picked up all the pens and pencils which were lying about on the desk. You used them to write a funny sort of book, without any words or phrases, a curious novel with a sulphurous tinge. You became the poet of pain, the writer of a tortured, scorned, accepting, radiant love. And I was both your heroine and the parchment on which you engraved your story, and the inkwell in which you dipped your barbarous pen.

'Paper woman, I am going to fuck you with pens and pencils!'

Your threat didn't tell me anything I didn't already know, and I tried in vain to close myself against your sadistic penetration. But I was too wet, I had desired you too much to become suddenly hermetically sealed . . .

Already you were invading my cunt, not at all gently, and I hadn't seen how many objects made up the bundle you'd just stuck into me. One of them grazed me as it went in with its too-lively top. I didn't have time to moan: already you were forcing me elsewhere, and I howled. I felt the pencils (there were no doubt several of them) entering my arse very roughly, and you pushed them right in with an angry, passionate gesture.

Your face fascinated me. It didn't look like it usually did. You were concentrating on an aim which I guessed must be diabolical, and I trembled. I was tortured, torn apart by two pens which were too rigid, too thick, irregular and wounding.

'Another one here, and there too,' you announced and you did it. I thought I was going to split open when you sent the two marker pens to join their brethren, especially behind . . .

Horrified, I saw you scanning the tabletop, and at that second I knew that my calvary was only just beginning. My torments then became as much moral as they were physical. As each pen was added, I hoped desperately that it would be the last, and I feared the next torture . . .

Alas, my desk offered unexpected resources. You found the drawer and I began to shiver with terror. I then pleaded with you, clung to you, but you remained pitiless. 'Another one there, and one here!' I was stuffed fit to burst. The rim of my vagina was stretched taut, and I thought I felt it tearing; my arse was horribly painful and its fragile lining must surely have given way, because drops of a warm liquid which I thought must be blood were flowing between my buttocks . . . Just how many biros, how many pencils, how many writing instruments had you stuck into me?

You froze for a moment, stretched out towards me as I sobbed with distress. 'You see, paper woman, how you have to be fucked?' You took hold of the handful of pens which were sticking out of me, and wanked me with a circular motion which almost made me explode. Both my belly and my hole suffered through this manipulation. I felt myself dispossessed of even the most elementary dignity. I no longer had sphincters, or any control of myself, and I dared not imagine what would happen when you blew up this terrible dam, surely with a more than tyrannical hand.

Pain, anguish and humiliation made me weep . . . 'Look,' you told me, 'I am writing your rape. I am writing how you got yourself buggered by a fistful of pens.' And you continued to move about inside me, to even greater effect, inciting me with pain and revolt . . .

And then, suddenly, there was a truce. You had just noticed the paintbrush you had used earlier, lying on the table: the artisan of my trouble, neglected and forgotten. It amused you to test its power once again, and you set to work again, as before, with the same delicacy, the same diligence. And in spite of my double rape and my double invasion, in spite of my tissues which were stretched to breaking point, I was surprised to find myself vibrating once again under the magic tuft of hairs.

The pleasure which I felt in having my cunt titillated was

all the more intense because it was unhoped for. This time, I was able to clench on to something – I had my cunt and my arse stuffed full, and it was the first time I'd sucked my pencils quite like that. I felt them sliding into me, so suggestive were the paintbrush's caresses. I was still stuffed full, but not so savagely; I offered myself to be possessed by two simulated shafts, rather monstrous, rather stiff, but orgasmic all the same.

I twisted and turned under the paintbrush's strokes, and, interested, you encouraged my efforts with disturbing filth: 'Move your arse, slut, make yourself come. You're going to get your kicks in a literary way! Do you like that, having both your holes fucked at once?' I felt myself going to pieces. I forgot the awful things you had just done to me, the better to abandon myself to the mounting pleasure, when you added: 'What's more, don't you know it's a pity to have only two holes fucked when you've got three?'

I didn't really have the time to realise, or understand, that the fine paintbrush you were stroking me with . . . that its hairs suddenly interested you less that the other end . . . And you violated me again, but this time in such an unexpected, unusual, incongruous way that I was at first bewildered by this tearing sensation, this fleeting lancet-thrust running through my cunt.

It was difficult to localise, difficult to analyse, and as I began to climax I had already lost the sense of reality . . . A burning, icy arrow was cleaving me asunder, coming up under my pubis, breaking into my bladder . . . Suddenly, I realised and howled: 'No, no, not there! Not so far! That hurts! It's going to come pouring out!' Too late, too late, I gave way to a wet orgasm, an orgasm in tears and jets, incredulous, painful, rebellious, a sabbath which, for the first time in my life, made all my orifices take part, and combined, with my rancour, the gratitude which I felt towards you for having known once again how to defy the ordinary.

Courteously, you delivered me from my tortures, and I was at last able to snuggle against you, you who were powerfully erect, and sob out all the sorrows of a little girl who has been raped. Of course, with the tenderness of a Prince Charming, you found gestures to console me and make me forget what a horrible bastard you could be.

When I got down off the desk, I saw the story which you had just written, printed on my blotter: a few red drops, in two different shades of red. A bloody colour, to tell that I had loved to the point of being torn apart, and the brilliant vermilion of an ink which had come off and flowed, to bear witness to the fact that I had allowed myself to be pierced and fathomed to depths where no one had ever been before you . . .

9

Without a doubt, I enjoy flicking through the album of our memories, our follies and our pranks, and I am astonished at the number of them, for our life together was rather short. Not short in terms of time, since our 'liaison' (which is what that type of relationship is usually called) lasted several years; but short in the sense that we had chosen not to unite our destinies, and only to make them meet sometimes, for an hour or a day, for the space of a what was generally a spicily amorous episode, and we didn't want to have anything to do with 'love' except in the most physical, the most carnal sense.

The better to forget that we loved each other, we made love everywhere, often, and in as many different ways as possible each time. Successively, or simultaneously, we experimented with the power which each of us had over the other, and this simplicity in our relations always allowed us to avoid the agonies of passion, followed by its inevitable sickliness.

However, we did not confine ourselves within the walls of a secret, well-locked house; for I remember that from time to time the profound intimacy which reigned between us was more obvious, more tangible, in the very midst of society . . . And certain outings we had together seem to me eminently worthy of featuring among the most succulent anecdotes of our story.

Like the day when we went to the cinema to see a dirty film . . . The idea came from you, as was often the case, but I was absolutely behind it. I knew in advance that the production would be no work of art. But I was nevertheless anticipating a certain emotion to arise from this session, first of all because I was with you, and I had never experienced anything with you that didn't exceed the ordinary, and which didn't have its price. And then my sensitivity, which I confess is a little special, a little perverse, was already excited, simply at the sight of that seedy little local cinema which stood stiffly between two dark alleyways, with its windows arrayed with miserable photos and its billboards which were sorrowfully disgusting. This cinema X had a clandestine, guilty air to it, a look of dirty shadiness which threw me into confusion. No one waiting to buy tickets, or at least so few people . . . A dirty old man who'd smoked his dog-end down to the very last millimetre before making up his mind to pay and go in, two Arabs with black fingernails, stooping backs, shapeless clothes . . .

The woman selling tickets was of course fat and dowdy, and the corridor leading to the projection room smelt foul. I swam blissfully in all these sordid conventions. I even allowed myself the luxury of feeling a little ashamed as I went into that dark, hot, smelly den, where you could make out a great many more people that the semideserted front hall might have allowed you to suppose, and which echoed with the moans and hoarse breathing of the two giant creatures disporting themselves on the screen.

You pushed me towards the seats on the back row. I knew from experience that you preferred these seats, which were more discreet than the others, with no one sitting behind to see us. I had to disturb someone sitting on the first seat, next to the aisle; he got up obligingly, but made efforts to rub himself against me as much as he could as I squeezed past. He breathed in my face, and his breath smelled strongly of wine and tobacco; and that odour, mixed with the vague stale

81

smells in the hall – dust and sweat intimately joined – both disgusted and overwhelmed me.

I sat down right at the back, against the wall. I wasn't disturbing anyone; I took my time in removing my raincoat: I didn't want to plunge right into the action, straight away. There were still sensations to analyse before taking an interest in what was happening on the screen. I had missed the credits, which as it happened didn't matter much, seeing as the work we had chosen had so little scope, but I preferred to descend slowly into obscenity, by a series of steps, so as to get the most out of it.

For my own benefit, I went back over all the impressions I had experienced since we had come in from the street . . . The hall, the windows, the woman selling tickets, the customers, the corridor . . . The man, in the darkness, who had touched me with a harsh, burning, rough, nauseating contact . . . The seat I had at last sat down on was also a little rough, a little nauseating. I felt the dirt-stiffened fabric and didn't dare give way to it too much . . .

At last I looked at the screen. We were only a few minutes into the film, but some pretty funny things were already going on. A fine woman in a little top and a pair of panties with a strategically placed hole was taking her pleasure under the sink with a plumber who was visibly innocent of all premeditation and who hadn't even had time to take off his overalls . . . He was working on her with all the diligence and enthusiasm of a good tradesman, and she was cooing with pleasure as he filed away; her legs were thrashing about, her bum seemed to be mounted on springs, and her breasts were escaping from her lacy plunge neckline.

The movements didn't seem very convincing to me – they were too rapid, too jerky; the girl's affectations, with her 'Ahs' and 'Oohs', were so artificial I could have wept; and she had not a word to say about the high-spirited rodeo of which she was the object.

And then, no doubt to make it last, the plumber withdrew and left her to moan on her own for a while. She writhed about lewdly, with her knees about five feet apart, and her

82

crack gaping wide. Close-up shot. The pubic hair is sparse, for the sake of visibility; her flesh seems covered in goose pimples, as though it were affected by the cold. The view of the actress's intimate parts is so direct and clearly defined that they can't really be called intimate parts any more. Here they are, on view for all the world to see: a gigantic, reddish crevasse with its labia on display, glistening; a wrinkled bum-hole, darker but hardly any more secret . . .

She masturbates herself, of course – that was planned all along; her fingers flutter from her cunt to her button, pulling apart the folds of skin, sliding smoothly along the length of her cunt, strolling towards her bum-hole; she puts one finger into her cunt, which is visibly wet: it is shining; she moistens her clitty with the juices, and goes off again in the direction of her hole, still calling to her fucker with the yowls of a she-cat in heat.

Another close-up shot, this time of the plumber's prick. You can see that he's a specialist in pipe work. He's got his own large-bore pipe, I can tell you! That swollen shaft, with its pinkish, veined, knotty flesh standing out against the blue overalls, and the tuft of hairs at its base, really gives me a thrill. It's throbbing against the coarse material of his clothing, and the glans is bursting like an overripe cherry. I can see it gleaming under the spotlights, and a thin, sticky filament flowing out of it . . . It's a fine tool, no doubt about it, and extremely suggestive!

The woman is still writhing about on the ground, opening herself wide with both hands, stroking her own breasts and buttocks, rolling her eyeballs round in their sockets, licking her lips with a salacious tongue, and talking filth . . .

Obviously he can stand it no longer. He lifts her up, sits her on the sink, and takes off his denims, for the camera must now search out those parts of him which are yet innocent of all gazes and take a new angle on the scene. Now he is naked from the waist down, with his working clothes concertina-fashion around his shoes and his T-shirt too short to conceal his buttocks. He turns his back to us: he's going to stuff her standing up. She's got one foot on the draining board and the other on the cooker. He stands with his legs apart (or at least, as far apart as his trousers, trapping his ankles, will allow him) and the camera's voyeuristic eye settles on his balls, and my word they're beautiful balls – brown, velvety, toned up . . . It really makes you want to slip a greedy hand around them, to feel this alluring pair trembling to the rhythm of their own sarabande . . .

As I'm letting myself get carried away by these unoriginal but rather charming images, I feel your hand on my knee, now on my thigh, no, between my thighs . . . This hand is moving very fast, and they are very docile thighs . . . Your fingers become infatuated with the seam of my stockings, play with my suspenders, feel the softness of the flesh between the nylon and my knickers, and slide eagerly a little higher, a little further on, a little further forward, a little deeper . . . Are you there, my darling? Consider yourself welcome! I was waiting for you without really thinking about it, did you know that? Can you feel how wet I am? I really want you . . . Yes, put a finger inside me, that's an excellent idea. Wait a minute, and I'll make the task easier for you! . . . And I push myself forward, right onto the edge of the seat, so that I can spread my legs further apart.

On the screen, he's still fucking her. They've changed the camera angle, and the balls have disappeared from view. The lens has fixed on the slippery cunt, and the shaft of hallucinatory proportions sliding regularly in and out of it. This regularity of movement really gets to me. It's a rhythm which speaks more clearly to my imagination.

Whilst you are continuing to titillate me, I stretch out and touch your fly. What a fine erection! I marvel at its breadth, first of all measuring your big hard-on with my palm, then with my encircling fingers. I feel almost as if I'm present at a three-dimensional show: in front of me, there is your erection in length and width, and there it is in relief under my hand. It's very invigorating, as a combination of sensations!

The seat of my imagination, which up to now I would have

84

situated somewhere in my brain, has just migrated suddenly: now it's at the base of my belly, between my thighs, between my buttocks. There's a storm in my knickers . . . I begin to daydream with my vagina, to fantasise with my cunt. I writhe about on the seat whilst you continue to titillate everything within reach, coming in and going out, and rambling about aimlessly around my moistness and my welcoming places.

And what if I took off my knickers? It's quickly done: I just lift up my bum and slide them off with one hand, whilst the other is still enraptured by your prick, sculpting it millimetre by millimetre. Ah! I would never have thought that the soiled velour covering of this seat could put so much heat into my arse! My backside is naked and my pussy is open on the slightly prickly, slightly rough material, and that excites me in the extreme. I would like to be stuffed by a cock covered in a sheath made of furnishing fabric . . . That would drive me wild . . . The very idea of it makes me swell up all over – my breasts, my belly, my arse . . . Everything surrounding, protecting and defining my crack, every part of it takes part in this erection, becomes engorged with sap; I have lead in my perineum and a sort of urgent, voluptuous happiness all over . . . You'd better believe it: my imagination has taken refuge there in its entirety.

My clitty is raving, and my cunt is dreaming of you, of your prick . . . That lucky bitch on the screen is getting herself well and truly screwed, and I'm feeling completely empty! I lean towards your ear and confess my arousal and, quite unembarrassed, you invite me to come and sit on you. The suggestion takes my breath away. I'd never dare do that! And, refusing the offer with a shake of the head which is meant to look indignant, I glance furtively around us. There's no one in our row, except the fellow who groped me a while ago. Immediately in front of us there are five or six spectators, visibly excited by the film, but . . . what if they turned round?

You persist, placing a hand on my neck to pull you towards

me, and I try to resist. Are you going to use force, as you sometimes do? No, it's too risky. So your try the psychological approach: your hand lets go of me, and I follow it with my eyes, fascinated. What are you going to do? My word, you're doing a real striptease act there! With two delicate fingers, you have taken hold of the tag on your zip-fastener, and with a diabolical slowness, you are pulling it down little by little . . .

In front of us, on the wall, he is still fucking her, and he's even stuck a finger into her arse and it's making her sing . . . Next to me, in the half-darkness, your prick has just sprung out, scandalously pale against your dark clothing. I glance rapidly at the chap sitting a few seats from us, but you seem to ignore him totally; you are doing me the honours with your prick, with tentative, madly persuasive gestures. You are taking it gently out of your trousers, holding it at the base to show me all its rigidity and full extent. It's as if you're holding yourself out to me, pointing with your finger, and I'm losing my head, stuck between this gigantic prick which is still doing its work on the screen, and which has long been making me slaver, and the one you're offering to me there, so close to me, so tangible, so alluring . . .

My body gives in before I consciously give it permission. Here it is, lifting itself up cautiously . . . I try to make as little sound as possible, but the minimal distance which separates us seems interminable to me . . . I am almost standing in front of you, above you. We must take aim carefully, and make no mistake. No one is moving in front of us . . . I daren't look at the other fellow, at the end of the row . . . Gently, gently, I sit down again, and you guide me with a hand on my waist; luckily I have a wide skirt, which you have skilfully neutralised by catching hold of the edge of it, behind me.

I continue to move down on to you . . . When shall we meet? I have never placed myself so carefully. I feel as if I'm in a film, too, but a slow-motion one . . . That's it, I can feel you, I'm touching you! You are pressing lightly between my bum-cheeks, sliding off a little, and then I swallow you up, very quickly. The path was well laid out, but all the same, it's a neat manoeuvre.

Well, I never! A perfect fit! I am crazy with joy, and I want to run, to gallop on you, but my heart is beating wildly, I'm stupidly, terribly afraid of attracting attention . . .

I decide against any feverish activity, any fantastic horse ride although the action unfurling in front of our eyes excites me to it, with its ever faster rhythm. The plumber is sorting out a terrible problem with a tap in his own way, he's bursting forth into his client's conduit with fanaticism, and I envy their freedom of movement – for I, impaled to the hilt on your shaft, am not sufficiently bold to move a little, to move up and down again, and measure its entire length with an entranced cunt . . . Your hand, wanking me into the bargain, is putting the finishing touches to my excitement – my God, my God, what am I going to do? I need to climax, really need to, and it's as if I'm paralysed . . .

My belly is full of suspense; it's waiting for the signal, contemplative, tense, all its flesh frozen before the liberating horseback ride; and the wait goes on and on . . .

I'm still not moving. Then I feel that, little by little, I'm becoming unimportant, down there, and the revolution is being sparked off without me. My cunt begins to tighten, pumping away madly, it has wanted too much, hoped for too much to allow itself to be deprived of pleasure by an idiot like me, who no longer knows how to do anything . . . It is throbbing, sucking, breathing, palpitating, swallowing you up . . .

I am going to enjoy you, your thickness, your strength, your power, but I want to climax sitting still, frozen with terror, and in advance I can feel that the joy will be sad and frustrating, as though I had eaten something good without chewing it, without tasting it, and swallowed it whole . . .

And this sadness seems so absurd to me, this sacrifice seems so silly, that I suddenly give in to my lustful animal madness, to turbulent rutting, to my ardent loins. Here I am! Here I am! And I begin to fuck you with all the energy of my thighs which have too long been clenched together, my calves which have too long been held still, my pelvis which begins an amazing extravaganza . . .

Wank me, wank me, I'm coming at the gallop; how good it is to run like that, to fly like that, to leap about on you without losing you for a fraction of a second! This grinding of our loins is incredible, incapable of failure, fantastic . . . The heroic charge, and then, at the summit of the hill, the discharge, which is no less heroic . . .

I am petrified once again, but this time it is with ecstasy, and I remain like that, shivering, hallucinating, for a few moments, sufficient time to see the big woman on the screen stuffing her titties back into the lace top, and, much lower down, to stare straight into the still distracted eyes of the lad in front who turned his head because I made so much noise in my race, and missed none of the spectacle . . . So what, eh? He paid his money to see a girl three metres high getting fucked for an hour and a half, and he's watching me in the darkness. I point out to him with my finger that it's all happening down there, and he turns round again, regretfully. It's OK by me. I'm blustering a bit, but I'd prefer to go out before the end of the show, because I'm not sure if I'll have the courage to confront some glances in the light of day . . .

You accede to my wish, and we get up, dress adjusted properly again, although we are both a bit out of breath. When I get close to the fellow at the end of the row, he stands back to let me get past, incomprehensibly more courteous than he was earlier, even more incomprehensibly because he sends me off with an unexpected 'Slut!' I am already near the door, but I round on him and reply: 'Go fuck yourself!'

Strange to say, this laconic exchange of words succeeds in getting rid of the last of my embarrassment, and when I get back into the street by your side, there's a smile on my lips. Life is beautiful, I've got sunshine under my skirt and a tremendous desire to laugh, gambol about, sing . . .

A fine, warm drizzle is falling and the pavement is shining.

The light and the noise seem new to me, and suddenly the air in the town seems so light! I think I love you because of the joy you have just given me, and for all the rest, but I mustn't tell you so. I must pretend not to know. I must feign stupidity and innocence, and above all not be tempted to interpret a mundane desire to sing in the rainy city as a symptom of happiness . . .

You have taken me by the arm and, as I linger in front of a shop window, you whisper to me in that roguish way which is so typical of you: 'I've still got a hard-on!' Your confession amuses and arouses me a little. Is it true that I was perhaps a little selfish just now? What can I do for you, now that we are back in the harsh light of the boulevard, far from the dark shadows which guaranteed us, if not invisibility, at least a certain form of anonymity?

You don't leave me wondering for long. Suddenly, at random, you push me through a gateway and, once behind it, crush yourself up against me. 'Can you feel how hard I am?'

I run away, laughing, with cries of pretend terror.

The chase is Homeric; from sheltered corner to alleyway, from telephone box to a darkened pathway, I escape from you and you recapture me, overcoming me, embracing me, making me dazed, holding me to you, kissing my throat, running your hands all over me.

'Hey – you haven't put your knickers back on!' The discovery galvanises you into activity, and you rummage under my skirt with both hands. Help! Rape! Stop! If someone comes past! But hurried, indifferent, cowardly people are walking past the building where I am struggling, and I can hear the faint tapping of their heels fading away into the distance.

In the end, I enter into the spirit of the game. Battle is joined, and you're not going to have me. I escape from your arms, run into the street and rush, not thinking, into the first shop I come to. You come in, too, right behind me. I'm breathing very quickly; half of me is panicking, and the other half want to burst out into peals of mad laughter. A girl who is busy handing pins to her colleague, on her knees in the window redressing the display, reacts to our sudden, tempestuous entrance with a vague nod and an 'I'll leave you to look round', which says a lot about her eagerness to serve us.

Actually, that rather suits us . . . I walk over to a rail of dresses and you follow me, with a glint in your eye. I stretch out a listless hand to examine the styles, and you overtake me a little, take me round the waist and force me to walk round the rail so that we disappear out of sight of the salesgirl. Sheltered behind this screen of glad rags, you begin to play at exhibitionists, whilst allowing yourself the luxury of making comments which are all the more spicy because I am the only one who knows their real meaning.

'Look at that one!' you suggest. 'Do you like it? Do you think it would suit you? Well?' And you show me a really big, really stiff prick which is sticking immodestly out of your trousers. 'Do you like the colour? And the shape?'

Your sense of humour unsettles me sometimes. I roll my eyes, no doubt in a comical fashion, since you smile, to beg you to be reasonable, eyes which question you. 'And what if she comes? What if a customer comes in?'

But you really couldn't care less, and you carry on your monologue with a breathtaking self-assurance: 'It's big enough for you, isn't it? Would you like to try it?' and you start masturbating in front of me, facetiously, absolutely delighted with your joke.

The saleswoman's voice reaches us from the other end of the shop, and it makes me laugh in spite of myself. 'Yes, you can try it for size if you like. The changing room is at the back, on the right!'

Ah! You don't need telling twice! You take hold of my hand and drag me, push me inside and draw back the curtain (which is rather thin) on this flimsy booth. But surely you don't intend to . . .? But yes! You intend to do exactly that! With you, it's always as well to expect anything!

As I'm about to protest, you impose silence on me with an imperious gesture, and, very quietly, pointing to the object, you say: 'Suck me!' I tell you, this guy's mad. And as for me, well, I'm even madder than he is, since I'm getting on with it without further argument.

I sit down almost instinctively on a little stool ordinarily intended for heaps of clothes, and you stand in front of me, sticking out your pelvis a little, and without the shadow of a care you prepare for the delights of a rather romantic blow job. Docile but anxious, straining my ears for any danger, I take you in my mouth, rather less than eagerly.

You decide that I'm not moving enough, so you slide right into me. No – you're going in too far, you'll make me throw up . . . I give a little nauseous retch, which the girl must have taken for a question. Politely from the window, she enquires: 'Is everything all right?' and I can hear you replying, in an unwavering voice: 'Yes, though it's a bit short, perhaps . . .'

And then begins the most surrealistic dialogue, which makes me truly regret not being able to laugh or protest with my open mouth.

She: 'You know, they're tending to be rather short this year!'

You: 'Personally, I prefer them to be longer! Longer and more closely-fitted!'

She: 'Yes, they have to be tightly fitted; this season, the sexy look's coming back.'

You: 'Yes, and this one's too short and not sexy enough!'

At that point, I look daggers at you, but you're enjoying yourself too much; there's a malicious twinkle in your eyes and in the end it softens my heart. I try really hard to be as effective as possible in the shortest possible time; but it's almost as if you're doing your utmost to resist and make the farce last longer.

After a few minutes, the salesgirl, perhaps intrigued by our silence, returns to the fray. 'What style have you got?'

'Something roomy,' you reply, without the slightest trace of modesty.

She: 'Is it black?'

You: 'No, flesh-coloured!'

She, vaguely dreamily: 'I can't visualise it . . .'

You, very quietly: 'Just as well!'

I am beginning to get really worried. If she comes over, our goose is cooked! I stop, I let go of you, I'm too much afraid . . . But you're deaf to my entreaties. Your big body is in front of the curtain, barring my way. You forbid me to flee, and even force me to turn round. You bend me over in spite of myself, even though I struggle to resist with all my strength. You seek the entrance and suddenly stick it into me, with such a vigorous thrust that I almost cry out.

You explain in a loud voice, for the assistant's benefit: 'We're trying something else, is that OK?'

'But of course!' she replies, and with her blessing, you begin to ram into me like a madman. My God! But where are you going to lead me to, you horrible fellow? I'm sure that the curtain must be billowing out as if it's in the middle of a gale! Hurry up! Hurry up, ejaculate, and let's get out of here! There's something impetuous and torrid about your onslaught, and, in spite of my anxiety, I am surprised to see the images which excited me earlier, in the cinema, passing by underneath my closed eyelids. I forget the shop and the assistant, and I even forget you, you dirty bastard! I am in a kitchen, with a horrible plumber who can't believe his luck, and I'm being shafted by a deliciously big plumber's prick, and I can feel that soon he is going to send me off to the plumbers' paradise of burst water mains, all sorts of leaks, pipes of every conceivable bore, Dyno-Rods and vacuum plungers . . .

Screw me, Mr Plumber, polish me until I shine, pass me the cloth, it's coming, here it is, here it is, I've made the bung blow off . . . !

I think that this time, we trembled together. I stood up, smoothed my clothes, relaxed, and was quite stunned not to see you dressed in those blue denims which had so raised my temperature . . . You adjusted your dress too, visibly satisfied, breathing hard, and smiling sweetly.

As we walked past the assistant on the way out, you of

course couldn't hold your tongue. 'No, definitely not; we couldn't get worked up over it; we'll come back.'

'Have a nice day, sir, madam, and goodbye,' she replied, handing a pin to her companion.

Lazy, impassive little salesgirl, you are the one who without knowing it, had the last word. For the situation had certainly had points in its favour.

10

Of course, eventually you suggested it to me, and of course, eventually I accepted . . . Knowing your temperament, resolutely open to all sorts of experiences, resolutely curious, resolutely breaking down barriers and taboos, I might even wonder how come you didn't have the idea earlier on. Especially as, since you first of all had the benefit of a lively imagination, you were additionally privileged because chance had put me in your way: for I was so broadminded and above all so loving, so ready for anything; yes, you really were privileged by an insolent chance which knew equally well how to surround you with convenient relationships, and, whenever you wished, create the most favourable situations in which to realise your desires . . .

When you told me of your discoveries, the previous evening, with an old friend who had a real knack for business, and who was currently making a fortune from running an 'encounter club', I shivered as I caught the very special glint in your yellow-gold eyes. Something within me had just worked it out, something which knew you well and loved you too much. You didn't even have to explain, or ask. Not even the awkwardness of choosing your words, not even the embarrassment of being specific. At the same time as I gave you my consent, I made you a present of this very special

ntuition, this almost magical understanding which I have for
he things which concern you. I didn't say 'What!' or 'How!'
or 'Why?' I didn't even exclaim, cry out, or show indignation.
I merely asked, 'When and where?' in the hope of a single
reward, that of your intelligent, surprised yet vaguely
admiring gaze upon me: I who already knew, already accepted
and was offering you, with my absolute docility, my
simplicity, as a token of my love . . .

Everything was arranged. You had organised everything
with the jeering assistance of your mate the pimp. You took
me to see round the apartment – which was stylish, as it
had to be – where I would come back a few hours later with
my client. You showed me the little secret room where you
would sit, incognito, and watch our goings-on. You wanted
to be reassuring, solid: 'You see, I'll be there, and if there's
the slightest trouble I'll come and help you!' Paradoxically,
your kindness and your foresight caused me a feeling of dull
anxiety. It was true, and what if I should happen upon a
madman, someone deranged? And what would you call 'the
slightest trouble'? What would you consider normal and what
would you consider alarming? After all, I had already
undergone your diabolical inventions.

Seeing my doubtful silence, you judged the depth of my
anxiety, and added: 'Anyway, you're not taking any risks at
all; it's not just anyone. He's a big man in the medical world,
the head of a clinic, something like that . . .' You became
tender, but – perhaps for the first time – without success.

I ducked away from your kiss, feeling vaguely as if I wanted
to cry, a painfully unexpected feeling of rancour. 'Leave me
alone, you'll smudge my lipstick! "He" has paid for me to
be made up nicely – don't spoil the merchandise!' I left.
My step was light but my heart was heavy.

He was waiting for me in the restaurant we'd agreed on.
I don't know how he recognised me, but when my taxi drew
up outside he was already there, waiting to open the door
for me: one point in his favour. He introduced himself very
courteously, and took my arm to lead me to our table.
Without looking at me for long, he gave me to understand

that I did not disappoint him. He was tall, elegant, very much at his ease, not even old, not even bald, not even ugly. There was something warm about his voice, something gentle in his gestures, something serious in his eyes. A very presentable – and even rather charming – fifty-year-old.

My feeling of anguish returned. Surely a guy like him, with his job, must have loads of nice-looking women at his feet. So why pay a whore? It was worrying, strange. Or maybe it was a hidden defect? Worse, a neurosis, an unimaginable kink, which he couldn't confess to anyone, unless she was a forewarned professional who could listen to, understand and undertake anything. But *I* wasn't a forewarned professional!

I caught on very quickly as I savoured my aperitif, and I very nearly got enough courage from the alcohol to shout 'Stop! Stop everything right here! I'm not up to it!' But he kept on talking quietly, as if we knew each other very well, and gazing at me with his brown eyes, which also talked in their own way, and seemed to ask: 'Is something wrong? Don't you like me?' I thought it rather kind of those eyes to ask that type of question, and I soaked my sudden gratitude with a big swig of Kir royal. I found the strength to smile, and drank again, with newfound confidence. He smiled too. Another mouthful. Here's to you, my lad, and to the incongruity of this situation.

In the films they show on Sunday evenings (social and psychological dramas for adults and adolescents), in the plays which made Margot weep, in cheap novelettes (a whole world of escapism), a heroine in distress, in the grip of the diabolical temptation of the truth, wrings her hands and confesses: 'My fine and noble darling, I am not worthy of your love: I never worked in the factory in the nearby town; in fact, I've been a streetwalker since I was fifteen years old!' I was sitting at the dinner table, opposite a stranger, and I really wanted to reveal to him: 'You're going to be horribly disappointed, but I'm not a whore!' There's something intoxicating about absurdity. And Kir royal, too. All I could do now was drink until I was drunk, and that's what I did.

Luckily, the alcohol didn't make me lose all self-control. After my initial reserve, I really wouldn't have wanted to go straight into extravagance without any transition. This fellow was ready to pay a large sum of money (my vanity was like a cat with the cream, which suddenly set my head spinning as much as the champagne) to spend an evening with an 'interesting' girl, and I had taken it to heart: I wanted to deserve that adjective. He had perhaps been tempted to find me rather numb, so there was no question of allowing him now to think I was hysterical! I hadn't even started work, and already I'd developed some professional pride! In short, I did my best to be 'interesting', and charming, and even brilliant.

The conversation ranged over quite a number of subjects, and I was surprised to find myself enjoying it. And yet, the man I was talking to still remained completely correct at every test, in a way which was really rather intriguing. Not the slightest equivocal gesture, not the slightest word or glance to indicate that anything at all was going to follow. He had foresight and great style, and yet he was without stiffness (and I swear that the word didn't make me smile), with, as his only compliments, his glance, which was a little more lingering sometimes, approvingly, and his way of saying 'of course!', very convincingly, when I had just put forward an idea which pleased him. 'Of course!', as if he had already thought of it, and as if it charmed him that I should be thinking the same thing, and say it, in my own way . . .

During the trip back, in his car, he talked to me about his job. He was an obstetrician. I don't know why, but this revelation disturbed me. Surreptitiously I looked at his hands, those hands which had rummaged around in so many women's bellies, those hands which had relieved, delivered and tortured so many women.

'They told me you had children?' he said, turning towards me. 'Yes,' I replied.

'Did your confinements go well?'

The discussion was beginning to sound more like a medical questionnaire. Without showing how surprised I was (I was

97

mentally trying to urge myself to be brave) I nodded. 'Yes, more or less . . .'

'Naturally . . .'

His use of that word made me wince. What did he mean, 'Naturally'? Was it so natural, so obvious, so certain that deliveries should go well? His optimism disappointed me a little, and my feminist enthusiasm launched itself into an indignant tirade: he might be an obstetrician, but he still had only a man's point of view, one of those points of view which are resolutely dishonest, resolutely blind, so as to deny the pain and trauma suffered by women!

He listened until I had finished, smiled, and then corrected me: 'No, when I said "naturally", I meant by natural means. It was only a question; I was asking you if you had given birth by what people still call the "lower passages".'

'Oh, yes, by natural means!' I was really beginning to wonder. Surely he wasn't going to give me an examination!

'You see,' he went on, 'your opinion coincides exactly with my own. It is absolutely undeniable that women suffer pain. And the obstetrician must not only be a mechanic. He must also think about that pain, know how to study it, quantify it so that he can better combat it. The technology which we possess – monitors, for example – gives us only a poor idea of pain. Up to now, nothing is capable of analysing the anguish which results from the very special situation which a confinement represents. For years, I have been philosophically interested in this peculiar phenomenon which means that at the moment when she is giving life, the woman giving birth sometimes thinks she is having a brush with death. I am trying to define the exact components of this stress, in different ways. Unfortunately, I am not a woman myself, as you pointed out to me just now; I cannot hope to live through the experience personally and completely. But that doesn't prevent me from, let's say, 'putting myself into that situation', from time to time. That's why I have called on you. I need the assistance of someone who is completely open, who is absolutely accustomed to all sorts of . . . fantasies.' He punctuated his lecture with a sidelong glance, finding me impassive – a great feat of self-control on my part.

Now I am guiding him through the alleyways of a quiet district. He's standing at the foot of the apartment building where you're waiting for me, somewhere in the shadows. Mechanically, I raise my eyes towards the balcony of the apartment. Of course, it's in complete darkness. And what if you weren't there? And what if this fellow, in spite of his peaceable appearance, turned out to be a nutcase?

I'm still trying to reassure myself when my quack takes a suitcase out of the boot of the car. A suitcase! And not just a little attaché case, either, believe me. A suitcase. I hope he hasn't got the wrong idea, and thinks he's going to spend his holidays here! I've been employed for one night, one night only . . . And yet I bet it's not his pyjamas he's lugging about in that veritable trunk!

He catches me looking and replies, quite laconically: 'Just a few odds and ends . . .' Then he takes hold of my elbow and we go up the path. My throat is tight and I am trying to exorcise my anxiety by inadequate formulae which I murmur to myself without any real conviction. Let's get on with the adventure! It looks like it might be comical!

In the lift, I can hear my heart thumping. Can he hear it too? I daren't even raise my eyes to look at him . . . Here's the door. Just enough time to break one of my nails on the lock and we're inside.

Very quickly, I busy myself with a host of useless things: there are a few lamps to switch on, a flower to rearrange, a cushion to turn on the armchair. I forbid myself to think, breathe in deeply to calm my ticker which is dancing a jig inside my chest. Just a little longer, doctor, and I'll carry out my ante-natal breathing exercises without feeling any pain, and we'll be at the heart of the subject . . .

Right, I'm not going to back out now . . . back out and so put off the evil hour. Is this guy going to jump me? If he could just jump me, in a very ordinary, very vulgar way – oh please, God, make him jump me!

The eccentricity of this prayer, dictated by my panic alone, perks me up a little. My sense of humour takes over again, and I think I'm dying to laugh, but it must be nerves. 'Would you like a drink?' I suggest.

'First of all, I'm going to explain,' he replies, apparently very calm, very much in control of himself, which doesn't go very far towards reassuring me. 'We're going to take part in a little playlet, you and I. We're going to recreate the conditions of the delivery room. You shall be the midwife, or the maternity nurse, it doesn't matter which – the medical team, anyhow. All I ask is that you are credible. I think I can rely on you . . .'

I can't even find the words to express how flabbergasted I am. I devote all my willpower to appearing as impassive as a block of marble, and making my face completely expressionless. If he were to look at me too closely, he would see question marks as big as houses moving in the depths of my eyes . . .

But he doesn't look at me closely. He is now busy opening his suitcase. He takes out a whole range of apparatus with an orthopaedic look to it, which my lack of technical expertise prevents me from identifying straight away. And then, seeing him going off with his metal tubes, his forceps and his thongs towards the big smoked glass table in one corner of the living-room, the memory comes back to me: stirrups! He's happily setting up stirrups on the sheet of glass, transforming it into a gynaecological table!

I hope with all my heart that, from your little hidey-hole, you can see and hear everything. I would laugh about it if I wasn't so flabbergasted. You set everything up to see your lady friend getting well stuffed, to spy on all the filthy things a client might do to her when he's rolling in it and isn't stinting on the quality of the payments provided, and here you are in a maternity ward! It really is too funny for words. It serves you right. Already you were imagining me in a waspie, or in leather panties, with thongs all over me, or maybe – and why not? – locked up in a terrible chastity belt, pulled apart by chains, masked, gloved, covered in rubber . . . Well, look what I look like now: I've just put on the white overall he has handed me, and he hasn't even demanded that I get undressed underneath. It's I who decided to take off my dress, quite naturally and to be more comfortable, but I don't think he has even noticed! It's a bit annoying, isn't it?

Now he's showing me round his suitcase. 'You've got everything you need in there.'

I bend over and examine the contents and take a rapid visual inventory of the compresses, various bottles of disinfectant, disposable sterile gloves, a stethoscope – in fact, a whole panoply of appropriate equipment. I feel as if I'm becoming a kid again, and learning how to play doctors and nurses. This is almost paradoxical, because those childhood games always had something rather dubious about them, and ended up turning into a game of 'you show me yours and I'll show you mine', whilst today, I am playing the whore with a gentleman who, for the moment, has absolutely nothing dubious about him. How bizarre life is . . .

In his suitcase, there is still a sort of buttonless hospital gown, which he unfolds and places over the back of a chair, plus a white waxed cloth and a basin. I hesitate for a moment, and then take the initiative with what is generally called the energy of despair. Forward! I have to know how to invent what has to be done; I think this man is expecting a little imagination from me, a certain ease of adaptation, and the talent of an actress who is really convincing in her role.

Under his approving gaze, I finish setting up the table: spreading the waxed cloth over half of the glass sheet, and falling down into the basin which I have placed on the floor. I take all the paraphernalia off a small table and bring it closer to the field of operations; on it, I arrange the bottles and packets I have taken out of the suitcase; underneath an enormous packet of cotton wool, I find a pair of Scholl sandals, those flip-flops which midwives like to wear. I hope that doesn't last! Adios, stiletto heels. I'm going to slip into the skin of this character right to the tips of my toes . . . I put a pair of scissors into my breast pocket, and that puts the final touches to my theatrical costume. I turn towards

101

him, visibly available: there, I'm all yours, whenever you want . . .

What happens next adds to this complete mystery, but in busying myself I have forgotten my stage fright.

My client, who is still very much at ease, sits down on the sofa. 'You were offering me a drink?' he says, smiling. 'Perhaps I could have a nice cup of coffee, very hot and very strong, to get things moving . . .' And he adds, confidentially, 'I've been saving myself ever since I knew I was going to meet you!'

In my head, I can hear the metallic sounds of a slot machine, clicking in search of the jackpot. I don't want to understand, but the slot machine keeps on spinning, very fast, tinkling, singing, chiming . . .

The meeting was set up three days ago. What could he have meant by 'I've been saving myself'? I give a questioning glance towards the door of the room where you are watching. What do you make of that, eh? But the door refuses to be disturbed; it clearly knows no more than I do.

A cup of hot coffee.

I go off to the kitchen and, all alone, I suffer the torments of a sordid light which is illuminated little by little within me . . . Bingo! Bingo, alas! Regretfully, I realise what my nutcase in the next room is planning. Philosophy, let's see! Coffee-grounds have never looked darker. Like a saddened, tragic Madame Irma, I bend over them and discover my destiny, and my eyes cloud over with tears. Do you realise, you dirty pimp, with your eye glued to your disgusting peep hole, that this fellow asked for an intellectual whore, an 'interesting' girl, so that he could shit into her fingers? Do you realise that I have got dressed up, made up, done my hair and preened myself to listen to the ravings of a fanatic who is more of sick man than he is a doctor, who has prevented himself from defecating for seventy-two hours, just to harvest the fruit of his sacrifice in my hands? For a trial, it's a perfect success. Do you really think it's going to give you a thrill, in your hiding place, watching this black comedy? Ah! I'd have done better to go and prostitute myself on some disgusting street-corner! I'd have hung around like an honest hooker, with one foot against the wall; I'd have picked up some very ordinary fellow, a factory worker, for example, or an Arab. He would have followed me up the disgusting staircase, into the dark, sinister bedroom; he would have washed his prick in a yellowed bidet, and I would have given him a good old blow job, whilst, hiding behind the flowery hanging curtain, you would have had a good squint at us while you beat your meat. Wouldn't that have been better?

A high-class whore! Tell me about pleasure and invention! And to think all I had to do was recite Baudelaire and spread my legs – how naive I was!

I gather together the cups, the sugar, the coffee, my bravery and my disgust, and drawing one from the other, I go back into the living room.

My mother-to-be has got undressed and has put on the operating gown. Only the prick is sticking out . . . Get a grip on yourself, spy, in your voyeur's cubby hole – this is going to turn messy! . . .

'If you wouldn't mind getting into position . . .' And I point towards the table. He obeys immediately, apparently delighted with my air of authority. 'No, don't put your feet into the stirrups yet, we're not that far on. Have a drink first.' I give him a steaming cup of coffee, and I prop his back up on all the cushions I can find in the room. 'Drink it down very quickly, whilst it's hot.' And whilst he's doing that, I go off into the bathroom. Ah! My good fellow, this is not the end of your sufferings. No doubt you're one of those ano-masochists who like having things stuck up their bums – well, I'm going to please you. Just you wait and see!

Without difficulty, I find what I've come to look for: a device for douching the vagina, I think, since it's a woman who usually occupies this place, but what does it matter? Doesn't my client feed on precisely that: the ambition to change his sex, for the duration of a fantasy? And then I also find a cute little golden razor and a silk shaving-brush, which must know a lot about their owner's intimate parts. Cute razor, adorable shaving brush, I am assuredly going to take you into unfamiliar territory . . . Here's a bar of soap, too, and a little basin – now I've got everything I need. Perfect.

In the delivery room, I settle the mother-to-be in position. Feet in the stirrups, in the gynaecological position. Of course, it looks silly to start off with, but I soon get used to it. 'Don't move – I'm going to shave you.' Ah! He wasn't expecting that! The previous hussies he's played this trick on no doubt didn't bother with finicky little details like that. I can sense he's a little reticent. It's easy to guess that he's perhaps married, and that tomorrow it will be hard to explain to his wife why John Thomas and his sisters are completely bald.

He didn't have time to think, because I was already soaping his pubis and his balls with an authoritarian brush. Dear lady, you've got some pretty funny-looking cunt-lips and a funny-looking clitty, I must say. And as I go over it, as I go over it again and again, this clitty takes on proportions which I hadn't been expecting. Ah, so he does get a hard-on from time to time! That's reassuring. And it's easier to manoeuvre a nice hard prick than a sort of overcooked shellfish that you can crush between your fingers.

The razor makes an unpleasant grating noise, in spite of the soap suds. Take a good look, my darling, from your hide out; see how well I can adapt to new situations. An hour ago, I was a whore in a low-cut dress; now I'm a barber, shaving a man's nuts.

There: I've finished, and it's all clean shaven now. I even slipped the blade in between your buttocks, right up to the bum-hole, which was clenched apprehensively. The youngster must come into a bright, clean world.

So, how's my patient getting along? Have the labour-pains started yet? And I palpate a visibly swollen stomach with a none-too-gentle hand. The left side, particularly, seems sensitive. I can trace the shape of the colon with my fingers, and it's undoubtedly crammed full. Very promising. Looks like being a fine, strapping infant!

During the examination, my fellow makes eloquent grimaces. You've got colic? Very good. Very, very good.

'Relax: I'm going to give you an internal,' and I put a thin rubber glove on my right hand; a little dip in the jar of vaseline (humanity demands it – after all, we're not animals!) and I stick two inquisitive fingers into my swaggerer's bumhole, whilst with my left hand, flat against his stomach, I exert a long, conscientious pressure. Really think yourself into this situation, old boy! Make the most of it! You're going to pay for all men, all of them. All those who fuck us, knock us up, have a good time with us, those who pay us and those who rape us, those who soil us and those who seduce us. You're going to pay for the gigolo who's pulled off the job, the stinking louse whom I love, crouching there in his cubbyhole, you're going to pay for all the brutal gynae specialists who pierce us, abort us, sterilise us, cut us and sew us up, and who forbid us to cry out . . .

Seeing women torn apart and bleeding has made you lose your marbles; you've ended up imagining that these poor women get their kicks bursting their arses in front of you; you've ended up thinking they're crying out with pleasure, and you're jealous, aren't you? We'll sort that out for you – you did right to call on me.

I burrow very deeply into his arse, without gentleness. In fact, the child is presenting well. But it's not yet time. 'Another two hours at least.' It's a categorical warning, without the option of appeal. I see my patient rolling her eyes in astonishment, even a little in fear. 'Breathe! You must breathe – copy me.' And I give him the rhythm, the panting of a little dog, the quack's brilliant discovery to make the unfortunate egg-layer believe that she is doing something useful whilst she is in agony.

Oh, how delicious revenge is! The mad mother-to-be begins to pant in time with his intestinal contractions. His thighs are open, his arse is hairless, and his cock is demented. With the stethoscope, I complete the sham: what funny heartbeats, and what a funny foetus! I can hear a significant gurgling noise. This fellow is full of shit . . . 'Don't worry, everything's going well, but you must be patient . . .'

Every ten minutes, he will have another examination. I fix my eyes on my watch, and keep up a pitiless tempo. One hour and twenty minutes. A glove, and some vaseline. 'Relax, and breathe in.' With facetious index and middle fingers I feel for the head of the infant which would like nothing better than to move along the royal road I am opening up for it. 'No, no, don't push – you might tear your cervix. It's not time yet. Hold back!'

An hour and a half. A glove, and some vaseline. He's beginning to grimace horribly. 'Breathe in, out, properly. That will raise your diaphragm, and you'll feel better.'

An hour and forty minutes. A glove, and some vaseline. I don't think he's ever been attended so well before . . . He's twisting about very convincingly. Even so, I think he has less merit than I do as an actor, seeing as his sufferings are more sincere than my interest.

An hour and fifty minutes. A glove, and some vaseline. 'I told you not to push.' My word, I have to tell him off! . . . If he continues this song and dance, I'll make him calm again with a slap in the face. It's a very good method, very often used in maternity hospitals. Apparently it calms people down . . .

Two hours. 'The passage seems a little narrow to me, so I'm going to start dilating you.' There, old chap, that cuts into you, doesn't it? So, you wanted to play mummies, did you? Well, just you wait: I'm going to really spoil you!

The bulb of this douche isn't very big, but if I refill it several times the volume should be adequate. 'Don't lose the rhythm. Breathe in. I'm just going to leave you for a second – I want to be able to hear you from the next room.' I go back into the kitchen, looking for a big jug which I fill with warm water, whilst I can hear my madman's panting, interspersed with moans, coming from the living room. It's almost enough to soften your heart . . .

When I come back with my receptacle, I feel as if I'm surprising the audience . . . Yes, at least, my partner who thought he knew his part like the back of his hand, and whom my improvisations are actually completely disconcerting . . .

So, you wanted to make a philosophical study of the stress of the woman giving birth, eh? So take that, and tell me about it! And I give him the first squirt, with all the enthusiasm of a rapist. The warmth, volume and especially the pressure of the water torture my nutcase. He's going to understand all the agonies of holding oneself back. 'Don't push yet; it's not time.'

A second squirt. Ah! My filthy bastard, you enjoy making yourself constipated, and climax in advance at the thought of my face and my humiliation! Savour your luck, because you won't always happen upon refined women like me! It's difficult, isn't it, to hold yourself in when you've got your legs in the air? Clench your arse good and proper, my pretty one. You ain't seen nothing yet!

A third squirt. His belly has swollen up. Honest, you'd think he really was pregnant. Fat chance!

A fourth squirt. It's becoming really critical. He starts raving, begging, crying out . . . 'Good, so we're going to push now, but gently, very gently, and keep control of yourself. Go on, push, gently. You're not completely dilated yet, so control yourself.'

Oh, poor me! It's going to be hard to stop this calamity! The mother-to-be's waters break with an impetuosity I can no longer stem. A dubious-looking Niagara Falls showers me as it flows past. My overall is no longer Persil-white, but it's my feet which amuse me the most. The channel follows the shape of the waxed cloth, and as the waters fall they shoot into the bowl with a sound which exactly evokes a public latrine, and some very unsavoury splashes.

'I said "gently",' and I pick up a big pad of cotton wool and use it to stuff the breach before the threatened expulsion. That's not what a confinement is like! It lasts a long time, it hurts a lot, and it wears you out . . . If you really want to feel as if you're about to die, old fellow, you must respect the rules of the game.

'Breathe in, breathe in faster and faster, pant, pant again.' As he seems to be calming down again, I gently release the pressure of my cotton-wool barrage. My shit-scared patient has recovered the use of his sphincters, but I don't know if he'll hold on to himself for much longer. I cleanse the area

107

with sloshes of disinfectant, which of course torments his arsehole, and the poor fellow certainly has got a funny-looking one. I'm sure he's going to get a cramp in his bum, from clenching it so tight!

The need to relieve himself makes him go terribly pale, and his eyes suddenly have dark rings around them. I mustn't manhandle him too much. What if he had a weak heart? What if he snuffed it there, with his legs in the air? Hello, complications! Talk about the aftermath of birth.

But I don't lose my cool completely, or take pity on him. I've begun to enjoy the game. He must remember this, this birth. It must make him really sweat (and I was going to use another word, such is the role of chance in choosing our vocabulary!).

I amuse myself by titillating his membrane with the tip of my finger. 'You have a hard perineum; push very gently, otherwise it will split.' I am gleefully taking on the skin of my character, the skin of the sluttish midwife who seems to rejoice when the woman giving birth is in torment. Let's acknowledge that it's intoxicating to reign over the pain and relief of one's nearest and dearest . . . My nearest and dearest is very near, only a few centimetres away. I take a good look at his immodest posture, with even the tiniest fold of skin and the tiniest hair (if he had any left) open to view. And do you know, he's still got a hard-on! Even his nuts are erect. They have contracted into two very hard, very round, trembling little balls.

What if I raped him? What if I got astride him whilst he was writhing in the agonies of childbirth? Now, that would be a laugh! Fucking him whilst he's shitting, whilst he is at last bursting under the weight of my body sitting on his belly . . . I feel a curious excitement which no doubt owes more to the powers which he has delegated to me than to the sight of his congested prick. But he's the client, not me. It's who has chosen, he who's paying, and as for me, I must keep to the role which he wanted to give me. So let's keep within those limits.

Another glove, and another examination. The delivery is

ear. My patient has come out in a cold sweat. His teeth are
clenched and the skin of his buttocks is lined with great
spasmodic shivers. OK, little lady, be brave, we're nearly
here. 'Relax, slowly . . .' Oh! Yes, courage is definitely
what's needed, and not just for my patient, who – having
clenched his arse for three days and a long, interminable night
– has bruised the constricting muscles so much that relaxing
them feels more like tearing them than relieving them . . .

I need courage too, to confront this absurd, nightmarish
moment when I see his hole dilate, slowly, just as I have
commanded, swelling up, opening at last to make way for
a filthy, fascinating offspring . . . I am overcome by
dizziness . . .

Yes, philosophy, why not? Look at me, my lover, my love.
Look and see how I am proving my tenderness, my
attachment, my faithfulness to you today! Watch me, marvel
at my gestures and my seriousness, the seriousness with which
I am reciting my surreal text; see me descending into this
spiritual hell, the vanity of existence, the madness of men,
see me overthrow the great ideas, trample on them, shit on
them. The miracle of birth, the marvel of life, a nameless
load of bollocks! Take a single glance at this scene, and weigh
up its aberration, and draw from it the moral which you
cannot avoid: in the moans of a hybrid creature, male and
female, animal and genius, in the ignoble gurgling of its
liberation, in a smell of life and death, of warm stable-litter
and torn prey, with incantations and rites which I have
learned God knows where, I am delivering a lump of shit . . .

My client knew how to see an idea through. He followed
the metaphor through to the end, until deliverance: a long
jet of spunk which sparkled his gown with opalescent patches
. . . For a moment I thought I might present him with the
newborn infant, but then I decided that, really, my duties
did not extend as far as bringing up children. What's more,
this unworthy mother didn't ask for any news of the child,
and wanted only to unfasten his ankles.

I left him to recover his composure whilst I did a rapid
clearing-up operation. Down the bog with the kid. A quick

flush and goodbye nightmare! I roll up my overall into a tight ball, and it's not a pretty sight: I take a long shower and only go back into the living-room when my doctor has tidied himself up, and put his 'odds and ends' back into his suitcase. He makes a show of putting an envelope onto the chest of drawers, and turns towards me: 'You were perfect!' Then he honours me with a very cordial handshake and disappears with his walking maternity hospital in his hand.

Later on, I notice that he has forgotten the overall . .

Once the strange companion of my sabbath has disappeared, the room returns to its thick, silent atmosphere. I could almost believe that I dreamed the whole of this hallucinatory night, if he had not left behind this symbolically soiled garment, and this blue envelope on the chest of drawers, if he had not signed his passing with a little shit on white cotton, and a lot of cash in an envelope.

My God! So much cash for so little.

When you emerge from your secret cupboard, I am counting the banknotes again. The little session you've just witnessed has undoubtedly affected you more than you're admitting. You behave odiously towards me to conceal your embarrassment, and you grab the money with all the swiftness of a hardened street-urchin. 'Give it to me! It's mine. You can make do with your little percentage.'

I'm getting a little tired of this game you're trying to play. I've had enough of obedience, and I'm going to play the rebellious whore. And I throw the overall into your face: 'Take that! You've got that coming to you.'

You hesitate at this insult, stunned and speechless for a few seconds. Will you become angry, brutal, vengeful and physically violent? I defy you with an insolent look, a mocking smile. In fact, I will end up giving in to tenderness, for it is clear to see that you don't really know what to do, or what to say.

Poor, poor darling! Is it normal that I should want to console you for everything I have just lived through? Is it normal that I should try to relax the atmosphere with a peal of laughter — laughter which is a little forced, but which you

110

accept as a peace treaty? Is it normal that I should love you so much, quite simply? Don't worry, dear darling, today I won't give in to the temptation of the great two-hander, the scene of tear-soaked confessions, and if I am weeping convulsively in your arms, whilst dawn breaks over this strange house, I shall allow you to believe happily that it is the mad, inextinguishable laughter of a good woman overwhelmed by a night which went too far beyond the realms of the ordinary . . .

11

No, not that: I didn't want to play the whore any more! Neither the high-class call girl, nor the streetwalker. You weren't going to do that to me ever again. You had been disappointed by the experiment, since quite frankly the obstetric fantasies of the nutty gynaecologist hadn't excited you. 'What a shame,' you said, 'what a shame,' and as you appeared resigned, I felt on firm enough ground to try out a new initiative. I avoided your diabolical gaze, the exquisite way you pouted to show your resentment. What an actor, what a great tragedian. 'It's a pity that we didn't follow the experiment through to its conclusion . . . It's a pity, even for you.' You hypocrite, pretending to take my interests into account.

I made the mistake of smiling, and you pounced on this first sign of giving up. 'You have only to choose somebody wholesome, reliable, uncomplicated . . .'

'That's right,' I interrupted. 'And how would you recognise him, this wholesome, uncomplicated chap? Is it perhaps written across his forehead: "Free from all sexual deviations, tested and vaccinated"?'

'No, but it seems to me that if you were to look for someone in a much younger age group . . .'

'Oh, right! Now I see! After paediatrics, I'm to become

a nursemaid! And maybe if I get one whilst he's still in nappies, I'll find one who's still innocent . . .'

'You take the romance out of everything!' The formula was a familiar one, and you used it on every suitable occasion, and often on unsuitable ones too, for I couldn't see anything poetic about going to pick up some kid at the school gates . . . As I pointed out to you, you were becoming treacherous: 'Hasn't it ever tempted you, the thought of a nice little young man? That's not what you've told me sometimes!'

Oh, what a bastard. I hate it when people use against me the things I've let slip in unguarded moments of intimacy. And yet, I must admit that you were right: perhaps a nice little young man would be nice . . . 'But look, I wouldn't want you to be there – that would embarrass me.' My objection of course disguised my consent, and of course you understood it as such.

'No, I won't be there. Only a very little bit of me. A very little bit . . .'

'How do you mean?'

And you handed me a tape recorder.

And so, late one afternoon, I found myself in a noisy bar in a suburb of Lyon, not far from a high school. School was definitely out for the day; the average age of the customers couldn't have been more than seventeen.

I had got myself ready very carefully. It was useless to think of rivalling the bright young things who accompanied all those little yobbos, and on their own territory at that . . . I had deliberately ruled out trousers, blousons, baseball boots, anything which might suggest I was too sporty or laid back. It would have been clumsy of me to give up the privileges and opportunities of my age, to try and seduce an adolescent wearing blue jeans which I'm sure his girlfriend would wear better than I would.

No plunge necklines, daring pullovers or tight skirts, either. These days, men, even when they are still young, spit on the whore, at least when she is obvious. And so I opted for a trendy but sophisticated style, a showy elegance, just right to impress and unsettle a suburban kid . . .

According to his temperament, he would either be flattered by his 'conquest' or perhaps eager to shake up and humiliate this perverse-bourgeoise type which often revolts the little city hoboes. The important thing was that he should follow me, and later on we could decide whether he fitted into the category of 'fatalists-who-can't-believe-their-luck', or 'rebels-from-a-rotten-society'.

I ordered a cup of tea − tea is very chic, and very out of place in this café whose job is essentially to distribute Coca-Cola. I let it get cold, because it was hot, because I didn't want it, and because I needed an alibi to sit endlessly on this bench which was sticking to my backside, but which provided me with a vantage point from which to watch everyone who entered or left the café.

I saw them all: briefcases, satchels, haversacks, wallets: scribbled on, slashed, daubed all over, bearing lists of all the current kings of the hit parade, and the slogans of young people eager for happiness.

Wedged between the howling jukebox and the yelping pinball machines, I tried hard to keep my calm and my judgement, scrutinising each new arrival with a discreet but critical eye. Too old, too small, too dirty . . . Ah! That one there. Oh, what a pity, there's someone with him; his girlfriend won't let him go.

Johnny Halliday was braying away beside me, 'Abandoned . . .', and I was tempted to take this tragic racket for an imperative, a sort of divine warning sent to me by the most modern means, when I saw . . .

He was strolling in nonchalantly, with thick, very dark hair, his broad shoulders clad in a white T-shirt, and his jeans decorated artistically with ink (death's head and motorbike, with a few illegible hieroglyphics, or at least they were inaccessible to my too-modest, Anglo-musical culture). His jeans were well-filled, at least as far as I could tell from where I was sitting, for he had obstinately kept his back turned towards me since he came in.

He walked through the door next to which I was sitting, opposite the rest of the room. I could only glimpse his silhouette in profile. Now he was getting involved in a feverish, secret discussion with the café owner. His elbows were resting on the counter, and all he was showing me of himself was a neat, insolent bum, adorably delineated in his trousers. I hoped he would turn round quickly. But what if he was ugly? What if he had spots?

If he's got spots, that's it: I'm going. No, I'll give him a fair chance. If he's got more than, let's say, three spots, I'm letting him go. I gained patience as I made bets with the absurd, whilst my hairy fellow was, alas, walking away, still with his back to me, in the direction of the pinball machines, where he began to twist his delicious backside to the rhythm of the machine's ringing bells.

All I had left was a ruse involving the toilets, the entrance to which was next to these engines of Hell. Look out, I'm almost beside him, now I'm going to walk past him, I have to turn round . . . That's it, I've seen him! Not the merest hint of a spot, one hell of a sixteen-year-old, an unbearably pretty little Arab face, thick, downy eyebrows, at present knitted in hand-to-hand combat with this glass and metal trollop who is moaning and exploding at the touch of his fingers. He hasn't noticed me; but on my way past I have intrigued two or three of his acolytes, who are less passionately interested than he is in the rattling of the pinball machines.

I just take enough time to glance in the mirror and rearrange a lock of hair, and here I am again. Look, it's me again, sorry, don't put yourself out. (But yes! Put yourself out, stir yourself, you idiot, and look at me!) And this time, I stop for an imperceptible moment to stare at him. With his head lowered, grimacing with concentration, and the tip of his tongue protruding from the corner of his mouth, he still hasn't noticed me yet. How can I compete with this damned machinery?

Fortunately, there are his friends. They whisper to him, casting sidelong glances in my direction. They even elbow him in the ribs. Thanks, lads, that's nice of you! He lets go of the machine, twists his neck round a little, and notices me. Of course, I don't lower my eyes. I must say the

115

maximum number of things to him, only by staring at him. Since he is no longer clouded by this frantic machine, he has become very intelligent. He pretends to stroll over to the counter, puts a hand into his pocket, counts out some change, giving me the chance to speak to him if I want to.

I'm not exactly slow. 'Can I buy you a drink?'

He turns round abruptly, his hand to his chest and his eyes out on stalks, and asks: 'Who? Me?' And as I nod (I too am lost for words now), he announces without ceremony 'A Coke,' and comes and sits down opposite me, not without casting a brief glance of complicity towards his friends on the other side of the room.

Sit down, little rascal, and hold on tight. I'm going to show you that your motto, 'Don't touch my mate', is a complete heresy. For, if you really want to live the adventure with me to the end, I'm going to touch you, touch you all over! You seem to me to be eminently touchable. Whilst you were coming close to me, with your Coke in your hand, I counted your treasures again: your very straight, long, elegant legs, your narrow hips, a promising bulge in your flies, the nice-looking arms of a man who is young but already vigorous, an appetising neck . . .

Now you are right next to me, and raising your glass as if to say: 'Thanks, good health!' Your long, brown eyelashes alternately shadow and unveil jet-black eyes, and come down to caress the mat surface of your cheeks when you lower your eyelids. Has your beard started to grow? Not as far as I can see. Your mouth, which opens slightly to drink, is reminiscent of a beautiful pulpy fruit, and with a shiver of sensuality I can hear the sound of your white teeth clinking against the edge of the glass. A very cute mouth, but completely dumb up till now, and yet you must speak, you pretty little darling, for in my life there is a spy who is listening, a spy who is dear to me and whom I wish to overwhelm.

'I've never seen you here before . . .'

Ah! He's engaging me in conversation. 'I've never been here before – this is the first time.'

116

'Ah . . .'

I can sense that I surprise him. He has a way of looking at me which means: 'So, what do you want?'

I attack, pretty directly: 'Will you come with me?'

Silence. He looks at me, shrugs just one shoulder. Why not? And we stand up. I find this ease of negotiating very unsettling.

'My car's out there.'

But he's still hesitating a little. He no longer has his mates' looks behind him to egg him on. Finally, he gets in. He grimaces. Something is bothering him. 'Where are you taking me?'

'Back to my place; afterwards, I'll bring you back.'

'I warn you, I've got no money.'

'I shan't ask you for any.'

'Will you give me any?'

Pow! Get that! I hadn't envisaged that request, not for a moment. And all the same, it makes you think about morality, a question like that. It's a good job he said that to me in the car, out of range of that accursed tape recorder you've set up in the bedroom. It would have had you in fits of laughter.

'Will you still come even if I don't give you money?'

'Yes.' I swear he didn't beat about the bush. He didn't have to think about it – he replied very quickly and very clearly. I could have kissed him!

'OK, so we'll just get on with it, and we'll see afterwards . . .' I know my words are rather pitiful. They sound a bit like idiotic blackmail, a promise of a reward for good and faithful services. I take a sidelong look at my little Arab. Have my words irritated him? I wouldn't say so, and I'm almost disappointed. But, could I swear to it? His expression is a little enigmatic, faraway . . . Suddenly I think of Gide. 'Arabs, Arabs, camped in their usual spots, fires lighting up, smoke almost invisible in the evening air . . .'

'What's your name?'

'Djamel. What's yours?'

117

'Oh, my name's not important. You can call me anything you like.'

The journey passes in silence. I search in my head to see where I should start, once we get to the house. And in the end, I don't decide anything. Everything will depend on him, on us, on the moment. Let's admit it, I've got stage fright.

At the moment of getting out of the car, I notice that he has come as he is, with his hands in his pockets. 'Haven't you got a schoolbag?'

'No, I skipped lessons today.'

What's the betting that I've picked up the worst pupil in the school? 'That's not a good idea.'

He's so incredulous that he looks comical, and I can quite clearly understand what that look is saying: 'No, surely she's not going to lecture me on morals,' and I burst out laughing. He laughs too. We have just taken our first step into complicity. What worries me a little is that we understand each other by hints alone, and that certainly won't turn you on.

In the flat, he asks me immediately, without hypocrisy: 'Can I take a shower?' And as I show him the door to the bathroom, off he goes with that lovely, measured step. What shall I do, what shall I do? Shall I get undressed, or not? Shall I fix us a drink? At any rate, I should check that the machiavellian machine is still there under the bed, push the 'record' button, feel remorse, have a cigarette, pace up and down. I take off my shoes! This decision relieves me momentarily, as if I had just made up my mind to do something heroic.

Here he is again. His crinkly curls seem even darker brown because they are wet. Look, he's taller than I am, now I'm barefoot.

'How about a drink?'

'If you like.'

'A fruit juice, then. I won't give you any alcohol, because that makes your willie droop.'

'My willie!'

His expression is one of amusement, with a hint of contempt. The vocabulary no doubt seems archaic and very childish to him.

'So, what do you call it, then?'

Surprised silence.

'You see, you should tell me, it would interest me. I'm looking for words, lots and lots of words to write down. If one day I write about our meeting, I shall use your words.'

'Are you a journalist?'

'No.'

'Do you write books?'

'No, but I write a lot. So, what do you call it?'

Embarrassed silence.

'Well, I don't know . . .' Thoughtful silence. 'There's "prick", or "plonker" or "chopper" or "schlong". There's no shortage of words for it.'

'Wait, wait, say that again! "Schlong" – how do you spell that?'

His cheeks are puffed out and his lips pouting. 'Pfff! Me, I'm rotten at spelling.'

How charming he is, this boy Djamel. The worst possible pupil, I'm telling you, but surely one of the most handsome.

'Do you know that you are very handsome, Djamel?'

He laughs.

'Did you know that?'

'Well, you're not so bad yourself.'

Thank you, thank you, dear, delicious, unknown little hooligan, even if you don't really think so, your efforts at gallantry come from a kindness which completely wins me over.

'We'll close the shutters, eh, will that be better?' Without leaving him the choice, I go towards the window. Above all we don't want any harsh light on us, on our two bodies, on our two skins . . . I certainly wouldn't gain anything from the comparison. The conspiratorial gloom of closed Venetian blinds, through which a ray of light can barely filter . . . I have read Colette, you know. But I'm exaggerating to frighten myself. I'm not yet as old as Lea, even if my companion

119

makes an extremely presentable, though slightly exotic, Chéri . . .

Chéri is now craning his antennae towards me, and very quickly guesses: 'Don't you want me to see you?' He must be worried that I'm really ugly underneath!

'You've understood completely. I'm very shy. And what about you: would you like to see me?'

'Yeees.'

'Then say so.'

'I want to see you, Miss.'

'No, don't say "Miss".'

'I want to see you.'

'Well, I want to see you, too. No jealousy — one item of clothing each, OK? I'll go first.' And I unbuckle the broad belt I am wearing over my blouse.

'That's not fair — I'll be in the nude before you.'

I hadn't noticed that he was barefoot, too. Where did he leave his shoes and socks? Has he abandoned them somewhere between the bathroom and the bedroom to gain time, or because he was too lazy to put them back on, or because they weren't very presentable? I'm ashamed of my suspicions, especially as the T-shirt he has just taken off looks perfectly clean.

His chest comes into view, smooth and dark like a beautiful piece of earthenware, well muscled and tempting. I place my hand upon his chest, laying it flat between his two nipples, just as you might touch the flank of a thoroughbred horse — and my hand, which is usually tanned, seems very pale-skinned against his roasted skin. We are standing face to face, and he is taller than I am, much broader too, and yet he is so much younger . . . What marvellous shoulders! I just can't resist the urge to caress them, and I spend a long time doing just that, delighting in it. Silence. My God! The tape-recorder! Don't let this sort of silence take over, or you'll have an eloquent, vexed scowl on your face when you hear the results of your snare, and I don't like that scowl. There are moments when it is difficult to keep quiet, but there are also moments, believe

120

me, when it is difficult to speak, especially when you feel obliged to. Do you know of any worse torture than having to break and fill silence?

Fortunately, my partner's impatience saves the situation.

'Your turn, Miss!'

'Yes, but stop calling me "Miss". Don't you like me stroking you?'

'Yes. It's nice.'

He didn't look very convinced. I suspect that within him there is a terrible seed of machismo: he already seems very affected by the roles he has to play. Being naked in front of me, for example – that bothers him. And allowing himself to be caressed, too. None of that, my lad! You're going to learn what I think of that. I don't know if you're a virgin, but in any case I suspect your education has yet to be completed.

'OK, watch. I'm taking off my blouse.'

'And the skirt? Take the skirt off too, it goes with it.'

'No. That's not in the rules of the game. We said one piece of clothing at a time.'

'Yes, but you had . . . you had a belt extra to start with.'

So that really annoys you that much. I shall pretend to be conciliatory. If you want to combat prejudice, it's no good confronting it head on.

'OK, there goes the skirt. There: you've already got a glimpse of a real woman – do you like it?'

'Why are you wearing a bra, Miss?'

'Good grief! First of all, get your jeans off. Second, answer my question: do you like it? And third, why are you wearing underpants? And fourth, stop calling me "Miss".'

'Oh, for heaven's sake. Yes, yes, I like it, it suits you, are you happy now?'

'Well, to answer your question about the bra, I shall take it off. As you can see, it isn't yet absolutely essential to me. But I'm trying to put off the ravages of time as best I can.'

'Well, to answer your question about the underpants, if I don't wear any, I get my pubic hair trapped in the zip.'

'It follows nicely – no more zip, no more need for an anti-hair-trap device. What are you waiting for? Jump to it! Down with the anti-hair-trap.'

And, as he is still hesitating, sneaking glances at the edge of my knickers, with one strategic movement I free both of us — myself from the last fortification of my modesty (which is saying a lot of a few square centimetres of white lace), and him from that naive pride which forbade him from being the first to surrender . . . Now he's happy and relieved by what, in his pretty head, he believes to be my capitulation.

In his turn, he abdicates. His prick appears. It's the coloured, circumcised prick of a little boy who's started to get excited. He stays there, with his arms held a little way apart, dumbstruck and embarrassed. His spicy skin shines in the gloom. Looking at him, I forget that he's also looking at me. Admiration and temptation have silenced my timidity. I am alone at the edge of the world with this young god from a mythology with strange harmonies, this child-king of a legendary Baghdad, this little prince with dark eyes and an indecisive prick . . .

Sinbad, gentle mariner, will you take me with you on your voyage? I approach him. My arms are round his neck, my mouth on his ear, my belly against his, and I can feel his excitement becoming localised.

'You make me really horny,' I whisper.

I chose the form of words instinctively so that it would revive the dialogue, which had been killed off by his embarrassment and my excitement. Oh no! The tape-recorder has started off again!

'Oh, so you've got the horn, have you?'

'Dirty little bastard, of course I've got the horn! Look, put your hands on my breasts. Now, if that's not a hard-on, what is it? Touch, touch me, you see, you're making them stand on end . . . And again, wait, come here, come, closer, on your knees, I said! Look there, there! What do you see? Do you see it? What do you call that, eh?'

'A cunt . . .'

'Yes, me too. And what else?'

'A crack, a beaver, a quim, a twat . . .'

'Yes, but what about that? What do you call that?'

'A fanny . . .'

'No, not the fanny, that: look closer. Do you see, it's getting hard too. Touch, touch it, run your finger over it, can you feel it? That's my clitoris, my clitty. Say hello to the gentleman, Miss Clitty, this is Djamel. I don't know if Djamel has ever seen a clitoris get hard in his entire life, you know . . . Say, Djamel, have you ever seen that really close-up?'

'I've seen photos.'

'Photos, but what about a real woman?'

'No, never.'

'Have you never made love, then?'

'Yes, a little . . .'

'What do you mean, a little?'

'Two or three girls . . .'

'Two, or three?'

'Two, very quickly, at night in the cellar . . .'

'Ah. Of course, the cellar is not really the ideal place to track down clitties. And was it good with these girls?'

'No, not very . . .'

'Not very for them or for you?'

'For me.'

'And what about them?'

'I don't know . . .'

'Did you ask them?'

'No.'

'Good. Well, today, Djamel, shall we start from the beginning again, as if there had never been any girls, no photos, and no cellar? I'll show you everything, I'll tell you everything, and you too, you must tell me everything, absolutely everything you are thinking, everything you are feeling.'

'Are you going to write all this down?'

'Yes, if you like, it's so that I can write it down, and also it's for you, and for all the girls you'll have later on, perhaps in other places than in the cellar . . . First of all, come here, come on to the bed with me. Lie down. I'm going to caress you because I want to, because it's normal, because people should caress each other. With the tips of the fingers. Close your eyes, let yourself go . . . I'm running my fingers over you. There, on your arms, under your arms, don't move, don't tense up, it won't tickle any more if you relax. On the sides of your belly. It's good, isn't it? It makes you hollow your stomach . . . There, on your pubic hair. You have a thick bush, and I like scratching about in it. Ah! Look, your prick wants to prevent me. It's a nice prick. Do you know, I've never seen a prick as brown as yours? Under your balls, with the tips of my fingers . . . Tell me, do you like my fingers underneath your balls?'

'Yes, I like it a lot. It gives me a hard-on.'

'That's good. Let yourself get a hard-on. I'm going to make you get even bigger. Would you like me to take you into my mouth?'

'Yes.'

'I shall do it, but you must talk to me, encourage me, explain to me what it's doing to you.'

'It's nice, it's . . . very nice . . .'

'More! Talk! Talk or I'll stop!'

'No, no, don't stop, I'll tell you . . . It's the first time anyone has done that to me. I've seen video films of it, with my mates, and when I saw a woman sucking a guy off, it always turned me on . . . I can't find the right words, I don't know how to say it's so good, but I can assure you it's good, when you pull on it with your lips . . . when I feel your tongue on the tip . . . when you take it right down inside you . . .'

'You mustn't clam up on me, keep telling me about it. It guides me, it pleases me. I like hearing you. Afterwards I shall show you how wet it's made me, just listening to you.'

'It's good, it's good, it's great, suck me, suck me again . . . Oh, that's good . . . Don't stop, don't ever stop, I'm going to come, I can't speak any more, I just can't, but don't stop . . .'

Oh, how good it is to be young! I would have liked to do my job meticulously, make him rave a little (I'm afraid that

124

the tape running under the bed has hardly had enough to satisfy its hunger), and also to leave him with a pleasant memory. But already he's enjoyed his first blow job with all the speed of a bush fire, and his youthful impatience has just burst forth onto my tongue in a warm, slightly bitter flood-tide . . .

You'll have to excuse me this treacherous thought, my darling, but I feel that I have committed a tactical error, abused as I am by my experience of using too-precise coquetry to excite a man who's flirting (oh, very honourably!) with his fortieth summer . . . This hot little darling's sensibilities are on a level with his cock. I'm just an idiot with a short memory, forgetting my ardent adolescence, and his urgent, torrid emotions, which are satisfied as soon as they are experienced.

I listen to my Lucky Luke's breathing growing calmer (he's the man who shoots faster than his own shadow), with my head resting on his smooth chest. The tape-recorder is starting off on another noisy tack.

'Djamel, would you like to touch me and feel how much I want you? Give me your hand. Can you feel how wet it is? It's not just men who get hard-ons and get wet – will you remember that? Swear that you'll remember.'

'I swear!'

'And the clitty?'

'I'll remember it.'

'It's very rare that you don't please a woman when you touch her there. Touch it. Ouch! More gently . . . More gently still, it's very fragile . . . Will I crush you if I lie on top of you?

'Touch me with both hands, behind . . . Yes, there, there, that's my cunt, do you recognise it? Go on, put a finger inside, further in, two fingers, come out a little way, move in and out gently, often, for a long time . . . Did you do that to your girlfriends in the cellar?'

'No.'

'So what did you do to them?'

'Oh, not much. We kissed, I rubbed myself against them,

I got a hard-on, they lay down and I tried to enter them . . .
Each time I came before . . .'

'But they didn't guide you in?'

'No.'

'Didn't they say anything to you?'

'No. They were breathing fast, and they were moaning a
bit. That's all.'

'Keep on playing with my cunt. Wait, I'm going to touch
myself at the same time. You see, I don't know how to come
without touching my clitty . . . Ah, here's your prick again.
Are you getting hard again already? What a human dynamo
you are! The two of us are going to fuck now, and I swear
you're going to have a good look round, you're going to see
how it's made in there, and you're not going to stay sweating
on the bed . . . Are you ready?'

'Yes.'

'I'm going to stay on top of you, I'm going to take you.
Can you feel me? Can you feel me pumping away at your
. . . what was it? Schlong. Your schlong . . . Are you OK,
can you feel me enough?'

'Yes, yes . . .'

'So, gently now: I'm fucking you, and you're waiting for
me, nicely. If you feel yourself coming, warn me. I'm going
to go on wanking myself . . . How does it feel in there?'

'Good, very soft . . . wet . . . warm . . . wait! wait!'

'What? Already?'

'I can't hold on for long if you keep moving like that!'

'Yes, but if I don't move, I can't come either. We'll just
lie still for a minute. Breathe deeply . . . Ah! you know, I
want your prick, I really want your prick, you won't refuse
me it, will you? Are you going to screw me, eh? Will you
try? When you've been wanking, haven't you ever tried to
see how long you could last?'

'No, never.'

'There are a lot of things to revise in your education . . .'

'Yes, I know. Women get hard and they get wet, first the
clitty then the seduction. I'll revise everything tomorrow.'

'You're a well-motivated pupil. So, keep on talking, I'm

126

coming down on your prick again. Come on, tell me all the names you came up with just now.'

'What for?'

'For your prick.'

'Prick, chopper, dick, schlong . . . cock, rod . . . shaft, plonker . . . knob . . .'

'Keep going, keep going; don't worry about what I'm doing, I'm bringing myself off while you're reciting. Come on, some more!'

'But I don't know any more . . . It's all very well saying "don't worry about what I'm doing"! I can't, I can feel everything!'

'Listen, there's no question of you shooting off before I come, do you understand? You'll manage somehow. If I disturb the rhythm, that'll put a stop to everything.'

'Oh, it's hard . . . Stop! Careful, I'm going to spunk off!'

'OK, I'm stopping . . . Last stop before the terminus, agreed? You're going to help me to come, you're going to touch my buttocks, my buttocks and my arsehole, would you like that? Right, off we go again. I'm going gently, very gently. It's sliding in and out beautifully. My arsehole, touch my arsehole! Don't be afraid – it won't bite. Put your finger inside. No, not just like that – wet it first. Yes, wet it in there . . . Now put it in. You'll do that to them, too, the girls in the cellar. But gently, always delicately. Will you do it?'

'Yes.'

'Repeat it all, everything you're going to do to them . . .'

'I'm going to make them hard, hard and wet. Make their nipples and their clitties hard. Make their cunts sopping wet. I'll put a finger up their arses, very gently . . . I'll wet it first with cunt-juice, and put it in gently . . .'

'Very good. Very, very good. Perfect. And you'll let them ride you, and breathe deeply so as to wait for them.'

'I'll breathe deeply so as to wait for them . . .'

'Whilst you move your finger . . .'

'Whilst I move my finger . . .'

'You'll let them rub themselves on your knob as long as

they want to. Ride up and down on it, stuff themselves with it for as long as they wish . . .'

'For as long as I can, you mean!'

'Soon, soon, it'll be over, Djamel, darling, little prince, you've got the sweetest, sweetest prick I've ever seen . . . Nearly there, nearly there, don't take your finger out, it's too cute, I'm there, let go, let go and tell me, tell me everything!'

'Me too, me too! But what's your name, what's your name?'

Joy made him lift his head towards me; for a second, he looked at me with wild eyes, with a distracted, ecstatic look, and also with sorrow because his first real man's pleasure is anonymous . . . I shan't tell you my name, Djamel. I don't want you to shout it out at the moment of your happiness, I don't want you to remember it, it doesn't belong to you. In your eyes, I want to remain this unknown woman, with her bizarre whim, whose gestures and words and body, perhaps, will open up for you a path which you must follow alone . . . For me, you are Djamel, Mohammed, Ali, it doesn't matter, you are the stake in a slightly crazy wager, a fruit which is tempting and so easily picked, a little prince of the suburbs, a little Rasta with tangled hair, faded jeans, and when I kiss your mouth, I kiss all of your homeland, the regret for palm trees which you do not know, the pain of exile, the suffering of not being either from here or from elsewhere, the misery of dragging down the piss-stained corridors of ramshackle council flats, of fucking girls in the cellar without achieving victory, you whose dark gaze of the proud Tuareg was made to scan sandy horizons, and not heaps of filthy rubbish . . .

Djamel, Mohammed, Ali, little North African, ingenuous and sweet, stark naked by my side, you seem to have come straight out of the garden of delights, and I should like to tell you tales, for I am Scheherazade . . . But I shall keep my eloquence for another sultan, not so young or so pure as you, and whose lascivious ears enjoy listening to my improper stories, and I am only making love with you the better to make it with him, who will soon hear your sweet, timid voice and your wild breathing, captured by a sly machine. Without knowing it, you are the hero of a story, Djamel from the shanty town, an adolescent lost between two continents, my romantic and fleeting lover . . .

'Djamel!'

'What?'

'Your prick is made of velvet . . . Just like a pretty little animal with satin skin under my fingers. And it's docile, too: look!'

'Yes, I've not got much to complain about . . .'

'Another little ride? A gallop perhaps . . .'

'Why not?'

'This time, will you come on top of me? Caress me with it . . . Just with the head of it, there, only my clitty. That will open it up, you'll see . . . You have to say: "Open sesame!", if you want to enter the treasure chamber . . . Say it!'

'Open sesame!'

'Come, come, Ali, the chamber is open now, come, come forward. Come right in. Gently. Now withdraw. Right back to the entrance. Out again. Now back in. I can feel you on the threshold of me, I can feel the top of your dick parting my lips a little, forcing me a little so as to get back in. I like that a lot. And what about you: what can you feel?'

'I feel as if you are holding me tight, swallowing me up. I want to move . . .'

'Not so fast!'

'Yes, yes, to move fast . . .'

'Don't gallop like that, you'll leave me behind. You're going to leave without me, and I don't want you to leave me behind . . .'

'No, no, I won't leave you behind . . . Touch yourself, there. You'll see, I know the lesson off by heart, right to the tips of my fingers.'

'Oh, yes, use the tip of your finger!'

'Do you like it like that, with my finger there?'

'Yes, I like it . . .'

'Have I made you wet like I should, have I given it to you like I should?'

'Yes, absolutely.'

'Do I fuck you well? Do you like the way I fuck you?'

'Yes, yes, I like it very much . . . Move your finger, come in, move back . . . Rub me, rub me hard, I'm a magic lamp. Rub me hard, Aladdin, and you'll see a genie . . .'

'I'm rubbing you, I'm rubbing you, I'm rubbing you . . . I've got one of those big, big rods, hurry, hurry . . .'

'Keep on rubbing, rubbing . . .'

'I can't stop, I can't stop any more . . .'

'No, no, we won't stop, but move around in my arse too, if you want to see the genie!'

'Oh, I can see him already . . . And what about you?'

'I can see him too, yes, I can see him, Ali, I can see him!'

And to think I thought that kid was a lousy pupil!

I went back with him to that noisy café; the lights were going on and it was still full of life. Through the open door floated the sounds of music, shouts, of kids who were a little weary, a little sad. A little group came out. They recognised Djamel, sitting in the car beside me and not really knowing how to say goodbye. Without discretion, they bent down, stared at him through the window (how was it then, you lucky bastard?), and looked at me too, jeering, conspiratorial, indulgent towards my greediness as a well-bred, idle woman who had just treated herself to a delectable little Arab with her afternoon cup of tea. And that lewd indulgence was more unbearable to me than the most severe of criticisms.

'Well, so long then.'

'Salaam, beautiful Djamel . . . Do you know it's a pleonasm, to say "beautiful Djamel"?'

'A what?'

'Djamel, djemil, that means "beautiful" in Arabic.'

'You speak Arabic?' A gleam of interest in his eyes.

'Oh, no. Just a few words, like that . . .'

He opens the car door, gets out, regretfully . . . I was going to forget!

'Djamel! Asma!'

130

He turns round, comes back and bends down.

'What about the money?'

'I don't want any.'

Thank you, you lovely little chap, thank you, saha! So much simplicity, and delicacy too . . I watch his pretty little bum swaying off in the direction of the café.

He turns round, and he's back at my car window: 'But . . . I owe fifty big ones to the old woman in there,' he nods towards her, over his shoulder, 'and she's making a real fuss about it . . .'

'Here.'

I won't do him the insult of increasing the amount. He takes the banknote, opens his mouth, changes his mind and goes off.

And then he turns round again. Ah! He doesn't spare the false exits. His difficulty in leaving me causes me pain.

'So, won't you tell me it, then?'

'What?'

'What's your name?'

'My name is Lea, my darling . . .'

When I get back, I find you in the middle of listening to the tape, and I can see from your knowledgeable look that it isn't the first time.

You've got a funny smile on your face, a little tensed-up. I suspect that you consider the experiment rather inconclusive, and the recording frankly not very exciting . . . I open my mouth to plead not guilty (after all, I did what I could!), but you get there before me. 'He didn't really make you come, did he?'

Good grief, we're actually jealous! Well, well, that's really a bit strong! I am torn between indignation, incredulity and amusement, and I am looking for the most ironic words, the most treacherous intonations, and then, incomprehensibly, I chicken out, in a very natural way: 'Of course not. I said it to please him.'

My darling, my darling, my dear sultan, my desire to please you compelled me to deceive you with this charming little ragamuffin, and now my desire not to displease you drives

131

me to a second deception, a secret one this time, and one which is a lot more upsetting . . .

When I think that I tried to nip in the bud the burgeoning machismo of a sixteen-year-old kid, and that I am molly-coddling and encouraging the heartwarming but hardened self-pride of a mature man . . . So what am I doing, turning a blind eye to all these whims of yours, what am I doing?

This evening, you're not going to allow me the time to ponder for very long. Impatient to wipe away the tenuous imprint of a previous and perhaps too-exciting episode, you are going to run your hands all over me, fill me up, overwhelm me, plough me, until I beg for mercy, until my cries and sobs wipe off the whispers and sighs recorded on that spy-tape, which is still running in the darkness. And only the frequency I reach will be able to persuade you, by comparison, of your dazzling victory . . .

'La donna e mobile . . .' Verdi, I advise you to bring her back.

12

We had set off in no particular direction, with no particular goal, and the storm caught us unprepared as we were driving through that little provincial town, far from anywhere. It was a terrible storm, and within five minutes it had submerged the roadway and made it impossible to see through the windscreen. You had to slow down, as it was a winding road. You looked at me. 'What shall we do?'

And then, round a bend in the road, appeared the big, ramshackle house.

Through the driving rain, we could just make out the large name plate on the front gate. It said: 'Nursing home for the retired. Specialised clinic . . .' The lines underneath were in smaller lettering, and were lost in the downpour.

'I've got an idea,' you said, and you began to drive up the metalled driveway, lined with vast lawns with half-drowned garden chairs and tables, with umbrellas too, which no one had had time to get under shelter.

You parked in front of the front steps (in a space reserved for ambulances). Just from climbing the three or four steps to the front door, we were soaked to the skin.

Once in the entrance hall, you went unhesitatingly towards the reception desk where a pretty redhead was filling out forms. Completely at ease, as you always are (and especially

133

when you've got a female audience, and even more especiall
when that audience is nice to look at), you began your routine
With an irresistible smile and gaze, and a well-modulate
voice, shoulders moving expressively (you made a show o
shaking your soaked jacket with two fingers, as though to
dry it). 'Excuse me, Miss,' (that's an old seducer's trick
always using 'Miss' for any nice-looking woman who seem
over thirty), 'we're passing through the area and we'd like
to visit a friend, but we don't know his name . . .'

The redhead sits in surprised silence, hanging on your every
word.

'Yes, it was the brother of an old lady who used to live
near us, but, needless to say, she was married and her name
wasn't the same as his. I think he's here, and it would surely
give him pleasure to see us again . . .'

'But couldn't you give me a few more details about this
gentleman? His age, his family circumstances, any other
clues, his first name, perhaps . . .'

'His age? No, I don't know, but he must be quite old. As
for his Christian name, it's impossible for me to remember
it, but one thing I'm sure of: he was a bachelor, or a widower,
so he was quite alone.'

I listen to him improvising with a certain admiration. She
does too, but she doesn't admire you for the same reasons
as I do. Look at him well and listen to him well, pretty carrot-
haired lass! If you knew the joke he was playing on you, you'd
soon open your green eyes even wider!

In spite of all her apparent goodwill, Carrots remains
perplexed. You add: 'He had some sort of attack. He must
be partially paralysed. It's possible he's even lost the power
of speech.' You glance at me maliciously. The power of
speech! You're the one who deserves to lose it, you bandit!
I hope with all my heart that our hostess will look
disappointed and tell us that there was nobody there
answering to that description.

Now, fortune smiles on the brave. And so does the redhead,
with a broad smile doubly motivated by professional
satisfaction on the one hand ('Oh, yes, I see.'), and on the

other hand, by the personal pleasure which she is feeling in doing you a service.

'Is he Polish?'

It's more of a statement than a question. You have no choice.

'Yes, something like that . . .'

'Room twenty-two, second floor.'

And, as you are thanking her with a velvet look, she continues tenderly: 'He'll be happy, he never has any visitors.'

Going up the stairs, you amuse yourself with a few of your usual facetious remarks: 'I really like seeing women go up stairs in front of me.'

But I'm wet and I'm shivering. The adventure which awaits us has made my palms really moist. 'How many times do I have to tell you that I'm not "women"?'

The corridors are empty. Not a sound, it's the time when all the patients have their afternoon nap. Behind the door, I hesitate for a brief moment but you pretend you haven't even noticed. You put your arm round my waist to reassure me and to force me to go along with you, then you knock on the door and open it, discreetly but with authority.

The room comes into view. It's small and rather dark. It's a mixture of a hotel room (with its fabric wallcoverings and bed-canopy, flowered upholstery, and big soft armchair) and a hospital room (with its sophisticated bedside control panel, covered with buttons, levers, switches and plugs). In one corner there's a television set, and next to it, a chair on castors.

You step aside to let me pass, push me forward a little, follow me and come up close behind me again. The man stretched out in the bed gives an almost imperceptible start. 'Hello, Grandad, how's tricks? It's Father's Day soon, and we've brought you a present.'

His eyes are a very bright, almost transparent blue, and they shine in his bony face. He has difficulty in turning his head, as though he were held in a rigid corset. His arms are lying on the sheet, unmoving, perhaps dead.

You cross the room, and pull open the curtains. The rain is pitter-pattering on the glass, and the light which illuminates the room has something glaucous about it. A few details appear, which I hadn't noticed before. The sick man is wearing pyjamas. He looks very old, and his gnarled fingers tremble a little. I dare not confront his pale porcelain gaze again, his eyes which have settled on us with surprise, and interest.

Without bothering yourself with useless questions or ineffectual scruples, you settle yourself in. You push the chair on its castors in front of the TV set, opposite the bed, sit down on it and pull me on to your knees.

'It can't be much fun, spending all day long in there, eh, Grandad? So watch: this is better than TV.' And you set about undressing me. First my T-shirt, which you pull over my head as one would undress a child. I'm resigned, and raise my arms without complaint, and I get ready to part company with my bra too, as you are already unhooking it behind me. But no. An error of foresight. It's an underwired bra, very low-cut, and you play with my breasts, pulling them out. Now they are lying on two semi-circular armatures which emphasise their fullness and make them more excitable. You irritate the nipples with your thumb, and – in spite of myself, dying very decently of confusion in front of the watchful little old man – they proceed to leap to attention with a frightful impertinence. Away with you, you traitors! Now I don't know where to look. In front of me, I meet the old man's attentive, forget-me-not-blue eyes, and if I lower my eyes modestly, I see my own titties like two raspberries, ripening at your touch. Talk about a rustic scene!

But your gardener's hands have decided to conquer more secret undergrowth. You hitch up my skirt without any preliminaries. It's damp, and is sticking to my thighs, and it resists honourably for some time, then at last gives in under the threats (I heard a seam bursting!). My knickers don't inconvenience you for long: they end up joining the pitiful little rag of my soaked T-shirt, rolled up into a ball and thrown on to the floor.

And now you are strolling about on my lawn, flattened by the trip in the car and the contact of my panties, and you work at lifting the pile by raking your fingers across it. It's labour which pleases you, and you take your time over it; and so that the spectator doesn't miss any part of your zeal as a landscape gardener, you open wide the gates of my secret garden to him, pulling apart my legs with a grip which admits of no resistance, arranging my right thigh on the right arm of the chair, and the left on the other side.

Welcome to paradise, little old man. With your white hair, you look like God Himself. If you'd like to take a tour around your handiwork! . . .

With a thrust of your pelvis, you push the chair into the space between the bed and the wall, right next to the old grandad with the eyes on stalks, and who, despite the obvious stiffness of his neck, manages to turn his head towards us. The panorama seems to fascinate him. I must say you're a very conscientious guide.

Abandoning the surface vegetation, you venture deep into the thicket, into deep burrows, emerging only to plunge back inside, and this game abuses my reserve and begins to excite me. Little by little, I feel the last barriers within me giving way. A hidden spring, which you had cleverly discovered, has begun to flow gently. Look, old fellow, there's a fountain in my Garden of Eden, a stream of milk and honey which wets me all over, makes the gooseberry of my clitoris shine, gives my apricot a pearly gleam, and lower down waters this dark, greedy daisy which my lover is enjoying alternately bruising, satisfying and famishing.

Do you like seeing that? Does it remind you of anything? With your azure-blue eyes, you must have swept quite a few girls off their feet, screwed them, fucked them, laid them . . . And now you are there, unmoving under a sheet which is becoming your winding-sheet, and your hands are trembling . . . I'm afraid you may be cold, little old Pole, you who were once no doubt tall and blond and well built, who sang songs, drank wine, danced to Slavic tunes . . .

I'm afraid you may be cold, seeing your body already

caught in ice, seeing in your irises the reflections of an iceberg. Look at what it is to be a girl who does not have cold in her eyes, who is not cold anywhere. You see, beneath my eyelids it feels as if I have the bark of a beautiful chestnut tree, smooth and russet-brown, and bursting into flame. And between my thighs, it's a thistle prickling and burning, a burning bush, a forest fire.

Warm yourself on me. I'm a hot-blooded Latin woman, with amber skin, dark hair and a brown belly. Warm yourself by watching me; from now on I am immodest, turbulent; look! Inside I am red and burning like a burst pomegranate, like a sweet fig, like a red pepper, like a sun-fruit – and I want love!

I am going to have myself fucked in front of you, just as one might light a blazing fire in the winter to warm up a frozen guest. Follow everything closely, don't lose one crumb of the scene. You're going to flick through a souvenir album with us. That man, on whom I'm wriggling my incandescent backside, that could be you, a few years ago. Darker. And he has a more vegetative gaze, too, with the green light of a river running over moss, with a malicious ray of light playing across it from time to time . . . But apart from that, he can play your part. You were no doubt equally skilful in persuading women, equally proud of getting them worked up, and knowing how to overwhelm them with a wild, magnificent prick.

You see, he's just unbuttoned his flies. It really is you, you used to get hard like that, not so long ago . . . Warm yourself on your memories, grandad, warm yourself as you evoke that time when it felt good to be stiff . . . Warm yourself at my chimney-breast, where he is going to cast up a delicious brew, and watch out for sparks!

I stand up to give you free range of movement, and allow you to open your trousers and let spring out that root which I can feel swelling up under my buttocks. I took off my skirt whilst you were unbuttoning your flies. The old man, pale and shivering, is still watching us, with an acute watchfulness, and what seems like the silent cry of his entire being . . .

138

You take my arm and make me lie face down on the bed, across his inert legs. I can feel you behind me, searching for me for a second. And then comes the invasion . . . I'm so eager to welcome you that you have buried yourself in me up to the hilt without meeting any resistance. Ah, yes! I love this broadsword you're using to whip up my ardour . . .

Look, grandad, look how well he's fucking me! I'm clinging on to the edges of enjoyment so as to taste it for a while longer, just for a little while. I'm guzzling it down with an unspeakable pleasure. It's big, hard and supple at the same time, velvety, juicy, it's crackling inside me and setting all of me on fire. Can you feel how it burns, grandad? Tell me, is it warming your legs, having a nice-looking woman fucked like that, on top of you? Did you know that a thing like that must be good for rheumatics?

My belly is like a hot-water bottle, and my cunt is all aglow. It's better than all the poultices in the world. Doesn't it make you want to move, too? Listen, he's playing a symphony on me! Do you see this guy? He's the Chopin of love, grandad! It's the first time you're going to hear a polonaise played like that, with such a lively bow, with such a fiery trombone. Ah! He's conducting me with his baton, you know, and soon I'm going to sing along with him, sing the score he's composing in the depths of me, with a merry instrument . . .

Behind me, clutching my buttocks, you get your folklore mixed up and you're dancing with your pelvis and your hips. Your hands are gripping me, scratching me a little, manhandling me. And suddenly, I feel another hand, cooler, lighter, placed on my hair. Ah! grandad, so you want to take part too, associate yourself with it? *Solidarność*, eh?

Do you know that your hand on my hair feels good, reassuring, like the benediction of a white-haired patriarch who has lived a long time, and who might say: 'Love each other, my children, continue after me. It's the only beautiful and true thing there is.' I stare at him, worn out and content with this one gesture, with this modest victory which nevertheless leaves him out of breath, and I decide to surrender there, at that moment, with an old man's hand on

139

me to protect me, and an impetuous ruffian's prick in my pulsating cunt. I decide to let go, to die a little, to be happy, to climax at last, under the gaze of those blue eyes, under this Polish sky, poignant with nostalgia . . .

When we go back downstairs, the redhead doesn't miss a trick.

'So, was he pleased?'

'Very, very pleased.'

'Did he speak?'

'No.'

'Well, he will next time.'

'Oh, we shan't be back for a while.'

'What a pity! But in any case, we can still use your visit as part of his treatment.'

'I beg your pardon?'

'This is a model clinic. We treat certain obstructions of the nervous system by using audiovisual aids . . .'

'Oh, really?'

'Yes, we make our patients listen to the voices of their nearest and dearest, several times a week; and we get results.'

'So we've been recorded, then?'

'Oh, better than that. Each room is equipped with a video system. Your entire visit has been filmed. We'll play the tape back to M. Grocholski. Perhaps we'll be able to get some slight improvement in his condition . . .'

We must have looked odd, for she continued, 'Does that annoy you?'

'Not at all. On the contrary. Anything to be useful . . .'

13

Some of the memories you have left me of the times when we met seem less pleasant to recall, and yet, since I have sworn to be loyal, it would be dishonest to neglect them in favour of uniformly light-hearted anecdotes, or moments of complete harmony.

Contempt, annoyance and disappointment also form part of our story, and they too were able to give rise to a new form of complicity, in their own, rather bizarre way . . .

There was, for example, that day when I suddenly felt as if I was tiring you. I was as clumsy as an animal caught in a trap, whose wild thrashing about ends up bruising it even more. And, to punish me for this clumsiness (for that day you definitely didn't suffer fools gladly), you abandoned me deliberately, cutting short our meeting without even doing me the courtesy of being abruptly but preciously frank, and pretending some stupid delicacy of wit, style: 'I'm going away right now, for fear of staying too long . . .'

The terrible, double fear which then took hold of me, the shame of not interesting you sufficiently, and above all that of provoking such a derisory excuse: 'I'm going away right now, for fear of staying too long . . .', the humiliation of thinking that perhaps you imagined that I was going to believe you, the humiliation of not being worth the truth, of not appearing strong enough to bear it: this shame and this humiliation immediately forbade me taking the slightest steps to keep you from going. Trying to hold back the other person had never been in the rules of the game.

And for a long time after your departure – an inglorious one, needless to say – I still refused to consider that you were perhaps, if not the more unhappy, at least the more embarrassed of the two, as I refused to give the terrible beast which had just bitten me the too-eloquent name of 'grief'. I wanted to believe only that I had been insulted, but gravely insulted, with an insult which would no doubt call into question everything between us.

And so, to wash away the insult, to prove to myself that I could still both seduce and be seduced, to take base, petty revenge on you, I deceived you . . .

From then on, the adventure may seem to concern only me, and to have no place in this notebook, which recalls the two of us together. And yet . . . Yet I shall tell it to you all the same, for you played a not insignificant part in it, beginning with the one of instigator – oh yes, it was an involuntary role, but your responsibility for the business is nevertheless complete.

And then there was the role of destiny, that malicious creature, which made me encounter 'him' that day, the day after a sad night which I had spent cursing you half the time and dreaming that I was cursing you the other half of the time. And so I met 'him', and responded to his greeting with the same gestures of enthusiastic fellow-feeling; the conversation didn't go any further than that, because each of us was at the wheel of a car.

It was when I got home that I said to myself: 'Incidentally . . .' I didn't add anything – I already knew exactly what I meant. With the complicity of chance, which from now on was entirely devoted to my cause, finding out his telephone number was child's play. My call found him alone, and very nice. I was rather laconic: 'Look, I'm a bit down, why don't I come over and see you?'

'That's an excellent idea!' he replied with the conviction

necessary to make me go up several notches in my own esteem . . .

To tell the truth, we had been silently promising ourselves to each other for a very long time. But a certain nonchalance, a certain timidity on his part . . . But you, on mine . . . So . . .

That evening was a dreamed-of occasion, which would at once overturn that handsome, reserved bachelor's insolence, and the despotic power which you were beginning to have over me. Long live the revolution!

I didn't take too long getting myself ready: you don't need to be affected or sophisticated to clamber on to the barricades!

At first, my attack was a reasoned one. I parked my car under his window, from which he was looking out for me. He came obligingly to meet me, showed me round his house, was very civil, very engaging, offered me something to eat, to drink, and, as I refused each offer, he allowed himself to insist. He of course wanted to know the exact goal of my visit (that fellow and I had at least one thing in common: we had a lot of doubts).

'You really don't want anything? Isn't there anything you'd like?'

'Yes, you!' I replied, very quickly, in the same way as I would have shouted: 'Death to the tyrant!' The confirmation he was searching for nevertheless dumbfounded him for a brief instant. He was polite enough to disguise the confusion which such a prompt confession had caused him by going through a pantomime of incredulous greed. I was sensitive to these two forms of homage – his courteous will to ignore my brutality and, paradoxically, to pretend to savour it. He behaved with delicacy to the extent of taking me in his arms, and I was grateful to him for it, for I understood perfectly that my rapidity, after months and even years of quiet patience, might unsettle him completely. His lips were soft and skilful, and it seemed to me that my saucy mutiny was proceeding without too much violence.

He babbled words which were a little mad, unanswerable, to comment on the adventure which had 'befallen him' (it was his term), and I decided that once and for all I would take this bewilderment, which he just couldn't cure himself of, for an immense compliment.

We found ourselves on a sort of rather hard bench, which I supposed must be his bed, since there was no other room . . . Our excesses were rather severely limited by the narrowness and hardness of the seat.

After an embarrassed silence, he confided in me, as though he were confessing to the most abominable crime: 'I'm thinking of the sofabed.'

I jumped to me feet. 'Come on, let's open it up.'

He was visibly concerned by the lack of poetry in the situation. He began setting up the bed with an air of painful resignation, and I no doubt hurt him rather a lot by demanding that the quilt should be tucked in at the bottom, as I was a little cold.

When we had finished preparing our sphere of operations, on which I was premeditating one of the most important political acts of my existence, he took me in his arms again, holding himself back for a few moments in a way which he hoped would appear romantic, before capitulating and lying down with me.

I took advantage of this embrace to whisper in his ear: 'Will you close the shutters? I'm shy.'

The relief that I saw in his eyes and all over his face said a lot about his previous bewilderment. He agreed very quickly, his own timidity reassured by mine.

I couldn't stop myself thinking, at that moment, of *our* first time together. Despite my pleas, you demanded that the light must shine on my naked body, and I was offended by your caddishness in forcing me, picking me out in detail as if I were a horse you were going to buy or just simply mount; I was offended, too, by my own sudden docility, my passivity, my lack of will . . . I swore to myself that nothing would be possible with you, and that I could not continue long with a man who, from the very first evening, ensured his distraint on my modesty and my pride . . . You can see how one can be mistaken, and you can understand why, much later, with this very tender, very delicate boy, I had the feeling that I was turning you upside down, abolishing in a single second the splendours of an improper rule . . .

He was hotter, more insistent as he pressed himself against me, as though my confession of weakness had given him further courage. I could feel that in his own way he was celebrating the revolt which I had invited him to join.

I began to undress. As he watched me indulgently, without insistence but not without interest, it was easy for me to drop my trousers and cast off my pullover. I kept my bra in my hand for a few moments, like a banner, and then at last I dashed headlong into the ranks of the 'sans-culottes', determined to lead history's most fervent insurrection.

He too got rid of his clothes, and I saw his body for the first time: browner than I would have thought possible, rather small and stocky, well built, with rounded muscles, all the abundant hairiness of a well brought-up animal, and tender, gracefully arousing places – the crease of the neck, the shoulder, the thigh . . . He had a Chinese look to him, with an impassive slowness, and his golden eyes, with their exaggeratedly-dilated pupils, shone in the artificial gloom caused by the closed shutters.

I touched his hair. It was very fine, very supple and so stiff, all at the same time. I touched his cheek, which was still soft although evening was drawing near, his fleshy mouth, his appetising neck, and I thought of you. The pain was keen, fleeting like the pang which presages an attack of toothache. And I told myself that it would pass, as if it really was a toothache coming.

I lay down beside him and hoped my impetuosity was convincing. I wanted to say that everything would be OK, and to believe it. But in my impulse, as wild and clumsy as all the stammerings of all revolutions, I must have bruised one of his testicles. He gave an eloquent grimace, and I thought about you again, about your solidity, your turbulence.

More pain, another pang. It's nothing, I tell you, it will pass . . . We stayed there, he and I, for a moment, waiting for our sufferings to calm down, he not daring to move a hand to the place which I had just manhandled, and I not really knowing exactly where I felt the pain: definitely a toothache, the sort where you just can't decide which is the guilty tooth . . .

My sedition was beginning to take on the appearance of a field hospital. The first victim of my barricades was an innocent testicle which I had crushed before I'd even made its acquaintance properly. I was terribly sorry . . . And along with it, fallen on the field of honour and for liberty (for *my* liberty!) the valiant little soldier which, just now, I had felt rising up against my belly. It was a shambles.

'It's all so sudden, so bizarre,' blurted out my kind companion in his confusion, visibly saddened by this apathy which was now weighing down on him with such cruel insistence. And, as all men do in this particular situation which this most embarrassing and vexing of male malfunctions represents, he analysed the problem, demonstrating to me in a gallant but ambiguous way that I alone was responsible, since he owed his impotence to the too-violent desire which I inspired in him . . .

At that moment, I felt for him only the most moderate of appetites. I stroked him, his cheek, his neck, his hip, covering them with kisses which were, alas, in vain.

And yet there was a moment of mad hope, when he lay down alongside me with sighs of desire. I was welcoming, but all he wanted was to get at my ear, in which he whispered: 'I can feel that I'm going to tell you very quickly that I love you.' To hell with confessions! I didn't want anything to do with them . . . We weren't there to dally, but to act energetically, firmly . . . Now, these adverbs seemed to have lost their meaning and their value for my partner, who was too loving. The weapon which he was still hesitating to wield would perhaps have been enough to satisfy my thirst for regicide, but at the moment of boarding, which I aroused with knowing undulations of my hips, the troops collapsed once again.

So here I am, alone on the battlefield, with my bad temper

intact, scorned, unsatisfied, alone also with a vague regret, and the ferocious, seductive, terrible image of a cossack with yellow-gold eyes who doesn't know how to say 'I love you', but who stands with his sword aloft, beyond the combat . . .

This memory disturbs me, and whilst my unhappy companion abandons the attack and lets himself roll away to my side, discouraged, resigned to failure, I gather together all my strength to silence what looks a lot like compassion in me.

Halt! I am here by the will of the people . . . We know what happens next, and are clearly already worrying about it. What a pity. I shall do without the bayonet. My heroism flabbergasts even me . . . I catch up with my army, routed on the edge of the bed. Fie upon long speeches. A real warrior chief first gives clear-cut, precise orders, and so I say: 'Caress me!' As my little foot-soldier, made even more timid by his defeat, is stroking me with a hesitant and too-discreet hand, I guide him, with an authoritarian and madly indecent hand, towards the field of operations: I place his right hand at the base of my belly, and his left on my buttocks.

I am kneeling almost above him, and I hold my thighs strategically apart to encourage manoeuvres on a grand scale. Here's something solid, precise, concrete. My acolyte's catastrophe will not overcome my ardour. I am Napoleon on the bridge at Arcola, alone against everyone, against you, against him, and even against everything, since I am almost straddling him . . .

But how dainty he is! How did I get involved with an effeminate little man like this? He brushes me with circumspect fingers, and succeeds in this tour de force of avoiding me, in every place where he might force me. Go for it, soldier. I'm going to pull your ear, since I can't even pull your prick. Have courage.

Ah! I felt a finger brush me lightly between my nether cheeks. 'Come in!'

The order, proffered in tones which are perhaps a little peremptory, panics him. 'Where do you mean?'

'There!'

147

'No? There?'

I'm wondering what this lad is doing in my battalion. Good. Everyone can't be a marksman, that's obvious. He's not made for the artillery, so be it. Farewell, artillery. I appoint him a patrolman, and here he is, just as stiff and starched. Quick march, rookie! You're not going to do orderly duty until tomorrow, duty calls you! And, as my shudders leave him in no doubt as to the path he must follow, this operetta-Tommy, with a despairing flabbiness, attempts a faint-hearted reconnaissance of the area.

The siege is short-lived. The resistance which he encounters makes him rush back in hurried retreat. What shall I bet you that this is his baptism of fire? I must look surprised and, in a localised way, disappointed. He explains to me, displaying a faintly grazed index finger as though it were a war-wound: 'I can't, it hurts me!' No! The situation changes as fast as a Punch and Judy show.

I think I'm going to give in to dejection . . . How difficult it is to wield the standard of revolt! How difficult it is to make the people rise up, to motivate them, to instil the necessary ardour and enthusiasm in them. I shan't be singing 'La Carmagnole' (a revolutionary song) this evening. Where are you, my dear old soldier, my lord and hussar, my conqueror?

I can feel nostalgia and neuralgia coming. Here it is, the attack of toothache. Toothache, heartache . . . It hurts me to know that I have lost a genial bowman, a tireless veteran, a fervent partisan of any attack, a champion of charges and discharges, a firebrand, the life and soul of the company who has no fear of etymologies, a squabbler, fighter, a smasher-in, a batterer, a swashbuckler, a swordsman, an Atilla of love, who has left me empty and defenceless, but still eager for new battles . . .

My heart and my body are suddenly in mourning. I am like Andromache at the court of Epirus, tired, and alone, the inconsolable widow of a warrior whom she loved too much, who was too impetuous, too passionate . . . 'O Lord, it is exile which my tears beg of you . . .'

It's my turn to roll to the side of the bed. I've just

reinvented the Trojan war, the trio's war, when Hector is too far away, and Pyrrhus is ridiculous. My campaigns are over, my trophies and my chimeras are over. The hour of glory is past, and the brave men have gone away . . .

It's suddenly cold in the room. It's the retreat from Russia, with the silence of icy wastes between the two derisory heroes of a failed vengeance . . . Waterloo, Waterloo, dismal plain . . .

The sudden action has failed lamentably and, with my nose to the wall, I begin to mourn the fact, obstinately deaf to this triumphal symphony which would like to burst forth within me. What a pitiful insurgent I make.

Behind me, a feeble sigh disturbs the unfathomable depths of my reveries. I thought I was alone on Saint Helena. Are you back again, little soldier? I haven't got the heart for conquest any more, you know – how about you? Nor have you, or so it seems. I have led you into a strange sort of adventure – you who are so gentle, so affectionate, so delicate . . .

I'm overcome with remorse. I feel as if I've been very badly brought up, and am very dishonest. This meeting will undoubtedly leave you with a painful and slightly humiliating memory . . . It would have taken so little for things to work out between us. Look, it wasn't so complicated: can you see how easy I am, and open to all investigations? Were you afraid of me? Of my demands? Of my vivacity? And yet I am gentle, too, inside . . . You haven't even come in to see.

I love sticking my fingers into myself, everywhere. In front, behind. How the devil didn't you manage to get in that way? As you can see, getting in is easy; you have to pass through the door, push it a little. There's a little knack to get the hang of, a password to speak, a sort of 'open sesame' to tame. Follow my every movement; I'm going in, coming out, going in, coming out . . . It's easier and easier, more and more roomy, more and more soft . . . And if you only knew how good it is . . . There's nothing more voluptuous than the arsehole, when you speak its language. After a moment, you don't have to do anything else, it gets by all on its own. Watch carefully: I place my finger on it, very lightly, without forcing it. Abracadabra! It's magic! It's disappeared! Cute, eh?

Inside, it's pumping away hard . . . You can play with the walls of it. You can enlarge them, push against them. It's absolutely delicious. If you push towards the back, it gives you the shivers. You feel as if your arse is bursting all on its own. It's a real turn-on. It makes you want to be really and truly disgusting; it waves two fingers at all the taboos in the world; it goes back to time immemorial, when we were unrestrained animals, unrestricted babies, happy to relieve ourselves no matter where, no matter how . . . The principles of hygiene and modesty have closed our arseholes tight shut for all our lifetime. Forbidden, not allowed, repugnant, forever hidden, forever shameful.

As for me, I ram my finger up my arsehole as if I was sucking my thumb, with the same defiant enjoyment, the same happiness at rediscovering a childish, joyful, free, proud gesture . . .

And when I push forwards, it's something else again. It awakes other desires, other hungers, do you understand? Too bad about 'La Carmagnole'. I shall dance the capucine — do you remember it? It's that dance where you knock at your neighbour's house. I'm knocking at my neighbour's house, through the dividing wall. The neighbour is at home, and gives me her reply . . .

Ah! Soldier! Forget Waterloo, come back to Austerlitz, I'm wanking myself everywhere, everywhere, do you hear me? Can you hear how loudly I'm breathing, how much pleasure I'm giving myself? I want to be fucked, little soldier, I want a big gun-barrel, a terrible cannonade, with red-hot shot, I want to be raked with machine-gun fire . . . Too bad, too bad, I'm going to resort to fighting with my bare hands, but what a shame that your rifle's at half-cock, soldier — I'd have guzzled it down with such pleasure.

The magic of language, the miracle of words, the marvel of briskly effective poetry! What my caresses couldn't obtain now happens quite naturally, at the moment when I'm least expecting it: my recruit suddenly leaps between my knees, like a real joker, with his cock to the fore. 'Use it! Go on – use it!'

Too late, little infantryman, too late, I'm already coming. But come in anyway, it's well meant. Let fly the salvo of a victory which is a little late in coming, but which will at least leave us with a charming impression.

The fall of the Bastille won't happen today, and it isn't for the two of us, but it would have been a pity to abandon the battlefield without a few shots being fired.

Goodbye, companion, no hard feelings. I shall soon rally another banner, wilder and harder, and which I regretted as soon as I had betrayed it . . .

As I pulled the door closed behind me that evening, saying farewell to my lover of fifteen seconds, I knew that in him I was saluting all the little, obscure, other ranks, all those whom a fearless captain consigned, with a kick of his hussar's boot and a thrust of his reckless sword, to the shadows of anonymous banality.

And, having come to celebrate the putsch of the century, I left with the sad disgust of a repentant deserter in my heart, together with the intoxicating hope of once more marching in step with the beloved rogue.

14

There is music everywhere. Falling from the ceiling, alveolate, luminous, futuristic. It bounces off the walls, stretched taut with a material which is thick, indefinable, moquette, wood, cardboard, a material which is at once hollow and warm, which resonates well. The music rises up from the earth and vibrates in your feet. You are entirely caught in a bubble of uninterrupted music, entirely possessed. The moquette-covered chairbacks you lean against are singing and trembling, and the notes come and burst in your ears, in your chest, in your belly. Through your elbows, resting on the table, you can hear strange frequencies which also inhabit the glasses and bottles and begin to crawl up your arms and right up to your hands.

Feeling the music with your whole body at the same time, being nothing but an immense eardrum, an immense drum which is definitely stretched, infinitely sensitive, and growling with each wave and each shock which reverberates across it, is a fascinating and intoxicating experience. It makes you forget that there are other ways to live than moving to mad rhythms, any way other than dancing.

In this nightclub you've brought me to, the acoustics are miraculous. Scarcely had I come in through the door when I underwent a fleeting metamorphosis: I began to become an instrument. Strings and brass and percussion all at once. First of all, I looked for the speakers, naively. Up there, perhaps. No, over here. No, behind me! On the ground? No, everywhere. Everywhere and nowhere. Chords, arpeggios, melodies come into the world through a gigantic and invisible speaker, which I am almost carrying within me . . . That's it, I'm pregnant. Pregnant with music . . . And I'm dreaming up hitherto unknown tunes, foreign scores, dreamlike echoes, archangelic trilling. The trumpets of the Last Judgment and the tom-toms marry within me, creating a bizarre, exciting mixture.

I abandon myself to this creation with its double meaning, this recreation of the universe, this recreation, this parenthesis in my life, this prodigious, dateless moment. I feel as if I am composing and being reborn at the same time, redefined by other criteria, rethought for another way of existing . . .

Everything here is made to facilitate escape and exaltation. The lights move, ripple, wink, dazzle without illuminating, surprise, hypnotise. These are the symbols of an artificial world, with fictitious stars, and unexpected colours.

Under these clustered lights, we lose our identity as we lose the colour of our clothes, our skin, our hair and our eyes. I have been looking at you for a little while now, fascinated by your phosphorescent teeth and your eyes, which are almost orange. I already knew that you were the Devil, but it took this descent into hell, a dark street, a blind alley, three steps down, a well-guarded door; it took this voyage into a world of shadows and cries, smoke and flashes of mauve lightning to uncover you as I had always imagined you: Satan in person, with flames in his eyes, and the bluish, inhuman rictus of this flesh-eating jaw . . .

Rays of light cross again and again to the tempo of a wild music, lamps light up, turn around, and a rain of little grains of light begins to fall upon us like electric snow.

My hallucinating eyes follow these sparkling atoms as they fall, and I am overcome by dizziness. I must admit that poppers have been passed around, and we have joined in the sacrificial rite . . . The magic vapours are beginning to have an effect – I can feel myself dilating to fill the dimensions of the room, dreaming of interstellar space and dazzling comets, whilst my body, still on the alert, receives and diffuses howling harmonies, an apocalyptic and genial clamour.

Suddenly, in the middle of the room, a large space opens up, its edges marked by the perfect circle of a luminous spotlight. The music has stopped, as if to prepare itself for a new, even more imperious, assault. A brutal, unexpected, incongruous silence which no one would dream of disturbing . . .

And suddenly, miraculously, emerging from who knows where, they leap on to the dance floor, as though propelled by the first cry of a curious instrument which begins to pant in the shadows. They are two tall, prodigiously beautiful black men. The brilliant white light illuminating them surrounds them with an unreal halo. They are positively dazzling, wild and bronzed in their opalescent casket, identically perfect in strength and suppleness. They dance to a monotonous, throbbing, barbarous chant, pulsing from a nameless, sophisticated, hybrid instrument, more computer than piano, but punctuated also by primitive calabashes. This joining of age-old sounds and new resonances gives birth to a timeless, fantastic climate.

First of all, the two men stand facing each other, like twins, absolutely identical from their short fleecy hair down to their solid feet which are beating the ground like broad battering-rams. They are naked, or very nearly so: all they are wearing are minuscule red posing pouches, as bright as wounds, more eye-catching than modest, which mark the base of their dark bellies with a voluptuous and bloody swelling.

I am captivated by their choreography, instinctive and yet knowing, which makes them leap up and down, crouch and leap up again, and move all over at the same time. Their shoulders, their outspread arms, their buttocks, their hips, their gleaming thighs, all made from the same beautiful steel, beat out a maddening, magic, irresistible rhythm.

Now they are miming a sort of powerful and graceful

154

battle, whose stakes we do not know. They seek out each other with their eyes, their hands, their feet, duck away, defy each other, come together and move apart, with a wild, passionate expression, a mask tragic with tension, a frown which narrows their eyes, lifts their jutting cheekbones, parts their thick lips.

Suddenly, one of them, turning round, slides his thumbs under the little string which holds his posing-pouch against his thighs. The fastenings give way with a premeditated ease. The cord was so tightly stretched that, at the moment when it breaks, for a fraction of a second you see two minuscule red snakes leaping up and lashing about in the air, and then it all falls to the floor – the living cord and the fabric.

The dancer, now totally naked, begins a series of frenzied leaps and as he turns his back to us we can glimpse, between his well-muscled thighs and underneath his statuesque buttocks, an impressive pair of brown testicles which are leaping about like the clappers of some mad bell.

The other man, who is opposite us, ostensibly succumbs to a theatrical hypnosis: his eyes are round and his mouth half open in a parody of terror; he keeps staring and shivering, staring at his partner's lower belly, at this prick which we still can't see but which we guess is wild and astonishing.

The wait goes on, cleverly orchestrated. I'm not far from letting myself submit to fascination, too: a fascination which is more discreet, but more sincere than that of the actor, on whose pubis the scarlet flower of a flaming eroticism is still blazing. I watch: only a few centimetres from our table, the gleaming shoulders of an ebony-skinned athlete, the rounded muscles which ripple along his back to the rhythm of the tom-toms, his arrogant, highly-strung buttocks, his tireless legs, and his sumptuous, immodest, insolent balls, so accessible you could howl because he finds ingenious ways to move welcomingly, lewdly, with his thighs apart and his backside thrust out . . . And what if I stretched out my hand?

To foil temptation, I take a little secret sniff of the ampoule of amyl. The spell works very quickly: this clandestine draught sets my imagination racing. I can actually feel them in the hollow of my hand – these two superb bollocks, continuing to move around amazingly. These balls really know their ballroom dancing ... I imagine I'm holding them, feeling their warm, moist mass, and using my thumb, I stroke their velvety envelope, erect like gooseflesh, and feel the two fruits which dwell within, hard, round, juicy, mobile beneath my fingers, terrifying.

I can hardly keep myself on the seat, and I feel as if I'm burning inside my knickers. In spite of myself I start moving to the same tempo as the dancers, and my pelvis follows the mad rhythm of their music, lifting first one buttock and then the other, very quickly, but very carefully, and this alternate, suggestive movement crushes my pussy against the velour-covered seat and opens up my arse ...

How these dancers are exciting me! And the one over there still won't turn round! And the other one's still got his G-string on! Impatience makes me catch my breath. I'm waiting for the sight of their pricks with a fervour at the limits of anguish.

Lost in my contemplation, I forget to look at you, but I know you're there, at my side, watching me writhe about. I press my flank against you, lean against you from shoulder to knee, savour your warmth and your welcome, and place my hand on your thigh ...

The fabric of your trousers lends itself exceptionally well to caresses, to investigation. I don't have to fondle you long to find what I was hoping for beneath my fingers: a thick cudgel of flesh, taught, swollen, vibrating to the touch, faithful and docile, meditative. I irritate it with my fingernail, from its tip down to its root, then, clouded, allured by the spring-loaded behind of the dancer who is still ignoring us, by his madly dancing balls, by the other man's tiny briefs, plump, visibly heavier because of a quite considerable something, I masturbate you under the table, so excited that I don't even think to unbutton your flies.

'Ah!' There is just one cry from the audience, and it is a little strangled, a little hoarse. The pleasure caused by the

rst rocket in a firework display, and what's more it's
ntimidated, and rather less innocent too: the naked dancer
as turned round. He is preceded, by quite a number of
entimetres, by a veritable column: it's brown, lacquered,
haken with what seems a life of its own.

With his belly thrust forward and his hands cupped
ogether under his balls, as though making some valuable and
eighty offering, he goes round the dancefloor in little
pasmodic leaps, maliciously brushing against the spectators
ith the end of this phenomenal hard-on, which sways about
 front of him without abdicating.

Here he is in front of us, very close, so close that I can
hake out the damp, purplish crevasse which cuts across his
lans, and, in the space of a second, I can imagine its depth,
s flexibility, and its taste on my tongue. The sensation is
o acute that it worries me . . . No more sniffing this evening,
r I shall go mad.

But the ballet suddenly changes direction and becomes a
rama. With the caricatured expressions of silent-movie
ctors, the dancers are now acting out a sulphurous story.
he combat and the defiance, interrupted for a moment by
he spectacular exhibition staged by one of them, degenerates
nto a sort of extraordinary chase. For these two genial
horeographers succeed in the remarkable achievement of
unning on the spot. The illusion is perfect. It's all there:
he foot pressing elastically against the ground, the thrust and
elaxation of the opposite leg, the effort made by the forearms
vhich in turn seek out speed and space, the sudden
novement forward which nevertheless ends up in the same
place. They are running after each other, madly, as if their
ife depended upon it, elbows to their sides, heads down, and
he tip-tapping sounds in the dark, accompanied and
sustained by the breathy hissing of a musical monster, a
hameless instrument which simulates breathlessness and
horror . . .

From the terror which you can read on the face of the prey,
from the sombre determination which characterises the
pursuer, with his rictus of cruel greed and his inexorable hard-

157

on, you can understand the argument: if he catches him, he going to fuck him . . .

Around the edges of the circle, the silence is eloquent. I our hearts, each of us is waiting, hoping, fearing . . . Hea still in a whirl after my little sniffing experiment earlie I lend myself to the game with passionate enthusiasm. tremble, I pant, and I flee with this dark, terrorised gian 'Run away! Run away! Run! He's coming! He's catching up He's going to catch you! He's going to screw you! Here h is . . .'

The distance separating them has imperceptibly diabolically, lessened. The hunter flings his hand forward once, twice . . . There, he's caught his prey. No, not ye he's struggling, escaping by literally flying away, and wit the effort, he loses his G-string which remains gripped in th assailant's hand.

Ah! The spectacle is worth a look! These men are definitel twins, right down to their pricks! Now they are running i profile, and the effect is striking. Their pricks are stil straining with a formidable strength, energy, and conviction and with equally magnificent rods.

Admiration and appetite give me pins and needles in m fingers, and shivers all over. I have found the zip-fastene on your flies, and you obligingly help me to carry out m extraction manoeuvre, arching your back, spreading you legs. I have taken your prick out of your underpants, whic hardly restrained it, and – still under the table – I faster on to it with an eloquent enthusiasm. It slips into my hand docile, a little sticky, and the touch of it finally bowls m over completely. I want to pull you off like I always do, want to manhandle you, wank you, hurt you, can you fee how fierce, impatient, demanding my hand is? I want you tip to be completely bare as far down as possible, I want to pull back your foreskin until it hurts, very high up, touch your pubic hair, pull on the envelope to stretch your shaft. make your glans swell up, pull it apart . . .

And then, very quickly, I put it all away again. Zipped up. sewn up, hermetic. I hold the foreskin very firmly, tightly:

158

you could tie a knot, make a little gift-wrapped parcel, with the big hard prick inside, ready to spurt out, like a fat banana in its skin . . .

No, it's not going to come out, I'm strangling it, and that pulls your balls forward, can you feel it? OK, I'm going to let go of the ballast, but gently, very gently. Millimetre by millimetre. It's devilish. The snail must come out of its shell as slowly as possible, I must absolutely control the situation at each fraction of a second. Captivating.

Little by little, little by little, I relax my pressure, and little by little the knob pushes and forges a way for itself through my fingers, dilating the orifice which I am holding firmly, and rises slowly in my ecstatic hand. Its head is now passing through, hard, round, slippery, and the skin is pushed further back . . .

Before our eyes, the terrible predator has at last leapt on his prey and thrown him down. He holds him in a crouching position, pressing down on his shoulders with his two powerful arms. The music is no more than a very faraway, throbbing drum-roll. Little by little, worn out, the victim gives up the struggle. He capitulates with his two hands which he places on the ground, and the other man takes advantage of this to attempt a greedy reconnoitre of the territory. With his knees on either side of the loser, he lets his eyes roam insanely, greedily, over his arse, swaying from one foot to the other the better to control him, and he holds still for a moment before the final assault, with the tip of his rod exactly between his partner's buttocks. From now on, this partner would be the total personification of submission, if it wasn't for the rebellious lance sounding a parley between his thighs . . .

In my hand, your cock continues its steady movement forward. Now I am gripping the base of the glans, which is poking out of my palm like an ace of spades, and the contact of the rolled-up collar which persists in coming down sets me aflame just as surely as the show we are watching. The triumphant hunter, certain of his victory, takes the time to ensure the capture of his prey: passing his hands under his conquest's armpits, he pulls him nearer, pressing himself flat against the arse which he offers, and celebrating his brutal invasion with a savage cry, suddenly he buggers him, thrusting right in up to the hilt.

I am living the scene in three dimensions: I have 3-D in my right hand, continuing to develop unconsciously. Once again I touch your pubis with my wrist: your prick is unveiled, incandescent, wet after this long striptease which has warmed and excited it. It disturbs me, holding it like this, beyond the usual, completely bewildered by this direct rape, in which the torturer and the victim continue to dance, one inside the other, punctuating their jerky rutting movements with a magical chant.

With a searching gaze, and a feverish attention, I follow the long thrusting movements of this mad Tamango, with tireless hips; from the distance which separates him from his lover, when he moves backwards yet does not withdraw from his backside, I can measure the ample dimensions of his battering ram. The other man is magnificent under torture . . . He has thrown back his head like a rearing horse, and on his belly his prick is throbbing madly, and on his face is written the wild expression of martyrs − a mixture of terror and ecstasy.

An infernal desire inflames me entirely. I would give ten years of my life to have my arse burst under an assault from that magnificent man. Everything in me is moving; I feel as if I am gaping wide, from calling out so much, in front and behind, especially behind. It seems to me that I'm wet everywhere, even there, and I'm not the only one. In my frantic hand, which has begun to pump your shaft violently, pulling its foreskin backwards and forwards, you have just left a thick, hot, viscous broth which drives me crazy, and conscientiously I smear it all over your prick, and what I can reach of your balls, your pubis, as if to glue myself to you . . . In fact, my hand does feel for a moment as if it is glued to your belly and, with an exaggerated drunkenness no doubt exaggerated by the poppers, I delight in the sticky contact of your spunk which is beginning to dry . . .

In the halo of light before us they are still fucking, regularly, powerfully, with more and more convincing, more generous thrusts. The prick of the man being buggered has become absolutely mad, and between his thighs it is beating out a regular, fabulous rhythm, and suddenly, just as the other man stops ramming into him and holds still, with his head thrown back and his eyes raised to the skies, this other prick bursts forth in an unctuous, generous flood-tide. I am almost astonished to see that his juice is white, coming from his prick of black marble. And how much of it there is! It was certainly worth running away like that, hypocrite, trembling like that, to get yourself screwed with this joy and an endless supply of spunk!

A perfidious jealousy is still tormenting my bumhole, and, whilst the actors leave the stage to damp applause (I can't be the only one with a starched hand), I remain with a painful feeling of frustration . . .

The lights and the music have changed . . . It is now almost dark, and the dust suspended in the air sparkles in the mauve rays of light falling from the ceiling. The tensions melt away in a languid slow dance, and I can hear the beating of my heart – which the previous show had rather overtaxed – slow down inside me. Shall we dance? I could hold my emotion, my turmoil, tightly against you, I could coax you, and maybe I would forget my unsatisfied hunger . . .

As I am opening my mouth to ask you, you place your hand on mine, imperiously and urgently. 'Look!' You haven't even turned your head towards me: you are staring at something, at the other side of the room, something which seems to fill you with enthusiasm.

I look for a moment in the direction you pointed out with a vague nod of your chin, and I soon notice her. She is superb. And she couldn't be more in tune with this exotic evening.

She is a tall, very affected half-caste, moving sinuously and languidly in a blue silk sheath dress, her naked shoulders caressed by the artificial blonde of her long vamp-style hair. I can see that she pleases you. She is dancing alone, visibly

satisfied with her body, with her dress which shows mor
of her than it covers, her breasts which are straining so har
against the fabric that you can make out their hard, excite
nipples, her supple waist, her rounded hips, her comel
backside . . .

Her belly is above all captivating, slightly protuberant
shaped with such indecency from the stomach down to th
pubis that you can make out the hollowed navel and th
exciting thickness of her pubic thatch, through the material

The acid fumes have given me all the audacity in th
world. 'Do you want her?' I whisper in your ear, an
your interested, almost incredulous look has rewarded m
already. Let me do it. I'll set up a magnificent fuck fo
you.

I thread my way through the swaying, interlaced couples
and I slip up to her, wriggling my backside and my shoulders
I'm there. Right up against her, smelling her perfume an
her body. She doesn't notice I'm there; she looks lost, in
world apart. I brush against her elbow and, as she doesn'
react, I place my hand on it. That's it. She's seen me. The
introduction doesn't pose any particular difficulties for me.
I show her the ampoule of drugs I've kept hidden in my hand.
'Fancy a bit?'

She shakes her head. 'No, I've got all I need . . .' But she'
stopped dancing, and is waiting to see what happens next.
Her voice is low, warm, but rather thicker than it is sensual,
and she smells a little of alcohol. So much the better, it'l
be easier.

'Have you seen that guy, over there?'

'The one sitting down?'

'Yes, in the red.'

'Is he a good lay?'

'I'll say he is!'

'Bring him to me in the toilets!'

What a peculiar universe! The extreme simplicity of the
procedure is almost a disappointment. I come back to you,
not really very proud of my victory, which has just been too
easy. With a wave of my hand, I invite you to follow me,

nd you obey without a word. You might at least try to look
urprised!

She's already there in the basement, checking herself out
n the mirror, leaning forward over a pink deluxe washbasin,
o that her magnificent breasts threaten to topple out. She
pots us in the mirror, and turns round. It really is a pretty
ace, surely rearranged and corrected by what they call
osmetic surgery, which makes your nose, eyelids, jaws more
egular whilst at the same time making them ordinary and
anal . . .

Her face is absolutely perfect, absolutely stereotypical:
lmond-shaped eyes, slightly oriental cheekbones, a little
straight nose, full mouth, with just the right degree of pout,
n oval chin . . . I have already seen this face a hundred times
n magazine covers, in the cinema and, of course, in a few
nightclubs like this one.

The introductions won't be difficult, between you (whom
I tirelessly spend my time with) and her (whom I already
know without ever having met her before). Maybe she's going
o ask you for money?

You look her up and down with a certain pleasure, caught
n the trap of her impersonal beauty, and I don't resent your
appreciation of my gift to you. She is looking at you, too,
and there is no repulsion in her eyes. Good, the initial
examination has lasted long enough, so let's move on to the
protocol of a cordial and absolutely courteous meeting.

I hesitate for a quarter of a second, for I suddenly realise
that I don't know her name, and that it is going to be difficult
to save face in these conditions. I can't say: 'Look, I'm
introducing you to this girl whom you were looking at a while
ago when she was dancing . . .'

It doesn't matter much, I'm searching through the
remnants of my intoxication for the courage to throw myself
headlong into the most preposterous improvisation you can
imagine, when she suddenly announces: 'Both of you at once.'

Good grief, never mind about that, I'm not saying no, and
I think that, since you are open to all experiences, you won't
see any objections to the plan. Our non-disapproving silence

163

simply encourages her to go on. Where and when? I hear you thinking, and I silently join in your wait. With a well informed index finger, she replies, just as silently, to our question. The dialogue is a brief one. We're not in a Cocteau film. Let's hope that the action, at least, will compensate for the film's defective soundtrack.

The scarlet-painted fingernail which she has pointed without the shadow of a hesitation designates a little adjoining room, a sort of open but discreet nook, quite dark, intimate, guarded by the semblance of a curtain and muffled with the dense greenery of potted ferns. There's no point in shilly-shallying – it's there and now. A quick conspiratorial look passes between us, and we follow in her footsteps.

In the alcove, behind the green foliage of the plants, there is a sort of wardrobe whose empty hangers reassure us a little as to the numbers of people who pass by this way; a large copper umbrella-stand which is equally empty; and a sort of indoor fountain, with complicated pipework. You'd think you were in the cloakroom of a smart hotel.

Our hostess, who seems to know the place well, gives a quick flick of her foot and catches the knot of the cord which holds back the curtain. Another conspiratorial look. Once the curtain has been freed, it screens off three-quarters of the access to the cubby-hole, which is in darkness once again. So here we are, all three of us, tightly squeezed together in the hot gloom of a room three metres long, sheltered from indiscreet looks by a curtain which smells of dust and mothballs.

This atmosphere intoxicates me. But there's no question of abandoning myself to the delights of the ambience: our companion, who clearly has a keen sense of realities and a phobia about wasting time, shakes us, constrains us, arranges us. 'You,' she commands, and her voice tells me she'll accept no argument. 'You're going to bugger me.' Joining deeds to words in a single second, she spins round, turns her back to you, quickly uses her left hand to hitch up the tight sheath moulding her body, thrusts out her buttocks towards you, and pushes me a little with her right hand to get hold of the

164

bar of soap which is next to one of the swan-necks on the sink, and the bar of soap disappears behind her, I assume so that she can anoint her most intimate parts, and it reappears just as quickly, having carried out its duties. She throws it neatly into the basin, where I hear it fall.

My eyes are still not really used to the darkness, and have guessed rather than truly seen all of that, and I'm still wondering about the exact itinerary of that bar of soap, and about your reaction, seeking out the yellowish flash of your shining eyes, when she touches me with an authoritarian finger: 'You, you're going to suck me off,' she announces, and, placing her hand upon my shoulder, she makes me bend and kneel down in front of her. This hussy sure is a quick worker. But in her haste there is also a reasoned organisation which I find rather seductive.

She twists round a little, awakening your desire with her arse which rubs against her prick, and I presume that you have already unbuttoned your flies behind her . . . As for me, I'm at her feet, between her delicious, regal, satin legs, which all my fingers are caressing with tingles of pleasure. With the upper side of my hands I move up the inside of her thighs, which she opens the better to receive us, you and me, and I reach her cunt which is still covered up by the hem of her dress. I roll the silken fabric up on to her belly, ready to uncover her grassy knoll and burrow my mouth into it, but you can imagine my astonishment when my fingers come into contact with a strange and rather stiff textile. What on earth is it? And yet, I glimpsed her buttocks when she pulled up her dress for you a moment ago, and I'd swear they were naked. A G-string?

I'm puzzled. In the gloom, I in fact begin to make out a white triangle on her swollen pubis. But what a funny texture it has! A little waxy, like a type of gum . . . Nothing to do with spiders, that's for sure. Perhaps a rubber fetishist? I try to find the elastic on these bizarre knickers, so as to get rid of them, but she moves away, thrusting back her pelvis to escape from me and at the same time offer herself to you, bending her parted legs. She keeps a hand resting on my head, telling me to wait. With her chin on her shoulder, she urges you behind to invade her: 'Go on, come in! Come in one stiff, deep thrust, right inside, I want to feel your balls!'

That's the sort of order which you don't repeat a second time. I can see you boarding her like a rough buccaneer. She has almost yielded, overwhelmed beyond her hopes, almost split apart. Clear the decks for battle! There's a storm in the rigging! Ah! Didn't you know the pirate, my girl? He has an efficient, precise rapier, as you will soon realise.

For a moment, I'm tempted to lift myself to brace her against the shock, for the act of boarding has rather shaken her, and you are now shaking her up with such a lively cut and thrust that she is surely going to fall on top of me! But in fact, she seems well accustomed to this sort of confrontation, and, once the first thrust is past, she has hardened her positions, standing squarely on her high heels, backside thrust excessively backwards so as to take full advantage of the rapier with which you're so joyfully running her through.

And so, what about these panties? I go back to my research, more and more perplexed. No cord, no elastic, no string . . . My hands grow anxious in their sterile searches. Good grief, this thing is holding on all by itself! I understand at the same time as she, with a brutal gesture, pulls it off with a single flourish. Rip! An enormous piece of Elastoplast, to hide what – well, I'll tell you! A damned prick which leaps out at the speed of light before my disbelieving eyes . . .

'Here! It's for you,' she (he) specifies, catching hold of my hair and pulling me towards the object of my terror. For a moment, I doubt my own lucidity. Have I perhaps sniffed too many drugs? My hands act as scouts, and all my senses are on the alert. I stare, sniff, feel, taste the thing. No doubt, it's a cock, a real one, with a pair of nuts, bald like the pubis (necessarily so in view of the Elastoplast) but in good working order, and rolling between my fingers, hardening, becoming round. The shaft is working too, coming, going, sliding, dampening . . .

It's a scene of madness which robs me of my voice, and that's just as well, because this nightmarish, Felliniesque creature, with breasts like melons and a goddess's bum, has just shoved its enormous prick down my throat, without leaving me the time to take the breath necessary to this type of exercise. A tragic destiny: I'm going to perish, stifled by the pitiless prick of this transvestite whom you're stuffing fit to burst, and you shall be indirectly responsible for my death, since each time you push into his arse, his prick comes and titillates my glottis, obstructs my trachea, and forces me to utter that stifled, convulsive barking noise which precedes nausea. Can't you hear it?

Stop! Stop, help, I'm going to die, or at least, I'm going to throw up there, on the ground, on the ferns!

A filthy business.

I try to resist, to hold back the enthusiasm which propels it into the depths of my gullet, but he holds me there with a fist of iron, violent, jerky, which says a lot about the sensations we're giving him – though for my part it is, alas, quite involuntarily. You are still stuffing him, and I can hear him almost panting like a woodcutter who's throwing in the hatchet, or rather the shaft, and I can feel your shockwaves through his shivers and swaying. That's too much! This jade is going to succeed in tearing out my uvula! Enough, for Heaven's sake! And with two decisive palms, placed on his pubis, with the thumbs down so as to get at his family jewels at the same time, I push him back and hold him at a reasonable distance, at last take a deep lungful of breath, and come to the surface with all the relief of someone who has just escaped from drowning. It's the first time that a prick has really taken my breath away.

This revolt isn't to the taste of my androgyne, who tries to force himself between my lips by thrusting his pelvis forward and grabbing my hair frantically. If he continues, I shall bite his prick for him. And as his agitation, far from settling down, seems to be transformed into fury, I pretend, though with a certain repulsion, to clench my incisors around this glans with which he is attacking me more and more

167

brutally. My threat doesn't have the effect I'd intended: now
this madman is beginning to grind his teeth and grunt in tones
which border on madness. 'Yes, yes, bite me! Take it into
you! Go on! Bite! Harder!' My word, he's cracked. Turned
on by amputation. But even so, I'm not going to shorten his
schlong for him. There are clinics for that. If you want to
get yourself a cunt made, go to Casablanca, old boy. Don't
expect me to do it for you.

Still on my knees, with my jaws clenched, and my forearms
stretched out to stave off the incursion, my hair twisted to
the point of torture, I form the most ardent vows for you
to come quickly, so we can get a long way away from this
hysterical hermaphrodite who is now twisting about like a
heretic burned alive at the stake. Alas, I don't know you very
well. You seem to be skimping on the job, not knowing how
to take advantage of the adventure if you gave in to pleasure
too early. You want to overwhelm her first, surprise her with
a robust, invincible prick, you want her to moan, tear herself,
beg, exclaim, go into ecstasies, pant, cry out, roar and dance,
dishevelled, on your magic wand. If only you knew, if only
you knew! For it's obvious that you know nothing . . . You
are still behind 'her', breathing into her hair, her undulations
making you giddy, working hard at stuffing her, and all I
can see of you are your hands on her breasts, which have
fumbled with the opening in her dress and liberated them,
and which are now manhandling them, crushing them,
compressing them with all the pleasure of a condemned man.

Ah! My darling, it's a firework burning you up, and you
don't know it. Hormones and silicone, the sorcery of modern
times, the still-babbling and already terrible alchemy of a
century on the march towards ambiguity . . .

If you knew that at the base of that belly you are trying
to tame vibrates a prick just like your own, that this creature
whose neck you are biting, whose breasts you are fondling,
whose arse you are stuffing in a masterly way, gets hard-on
as it feels the touch of my teeth, my tongue, my tonsils, is
pulling my hair so that I suck the most amazing cock in
history, suddenly lets go of my hair to guide my hands under

its inflated, trembling balls, flattening them there and demanding with gesture and word that I caress them hotly, feverishly, though I lack the impetus . . .

'Crush me!' he repeats, wildly, distractedly, and you, my darling, still don't know that this madman, this madwoman, wants me to crush his nuts with a sadism which is cruelly lacking in me . . . I feel so small, so disarmed, and such a pacifist! This guy hurts me with his pathetic quest for suffering. Is it necessary every time he wants to come for him to set up a simulated castration? I, who have sometimes wanted so much to have a prick, to force you with, to ensure my possession of and power over you, to enter your warm, tight entrails, and to feel you feeling me first, fearing me, then, little by little, welcoming me, making room for me, pumping against me . . .

What a sad life! What a sad life for he who denies it, refuses it, what a sad prick that prick is, strangled with Elastoplast, clandestine, squashed down, bandaged like a wound, thought of as a shameful illness. What a sad, suicidal prick which my teeth are grazing, which demands the guillotine of an expeditious, vengeful bite . . .

I haven't got the heart to bite you, you poor transvestite burdened with a virility you don't want, and which is paradoxical, incongruous. I haven't the heart to obey you, to crush your balls, to massacre you, to humiliate even more this thing which you are already hiding and scorning . . .

And yet what would you do with my compassion, you proud, pitiful monster, my half-sister, half only, much more beautiful than I am, but so much more fragile? . . . My hands are still hesitating on the verge of tenderness, and my mouth too, which, suddenly, she forgets to force, to throw herself into one of the most spectacular horseback rides imaginable. Her body heaves, staggers, starts, the whole of it overcome by fever, but still she does not climax . . .

And you, the male, the real one, are you going to hold out long at this fleeting pace? I worry about both of you, and especially for you, who may at any moment overthrow our order, try something else, another approach, in another position. I know your taste for variety, and the cunning ardour which you often deploy to bewilder pleasure. Beware of shocks, if that happens! Your reaction terrifies me in advance. And so when Carmen Jones, with a hand under my chin, tries to lift me up, ordering me: 'Come here! Turn round!', terror overtakes me completely. No! No, above all, not that! Surely we're not all going to screw each other now? I don't want to, I don't want you to see the truth, I don't want you to see yourself fucking a transvestite, I feel responsible for it all, for your surprise which you won't be able to disguise, for your loss of your erection, perhaps, and for the hatred in your eyes . . . for him? for her? What should I say? What should I do?

I am in a state of panic. Not screwed, but I don't care. The fire in my arse has already left me. I'm caught in the absurd trap of our too-great and too-illusory freedom . . . It's a nightmare. You're still pumping way behind her, salacious and innocent. But for how much longer? I struggle with all my body as I kneel there, as if to beg for a strange pardon. Have mercy, I won't do it any more, I didn't know . . . With a desperate hand I fight her wrist, under my chin. 'Stand up! turn round!' My other hand has brushed against my pocket. The ampoule is there, a little cylinder dazzling with hope . . . Thank you, God! A little sniff to save me, and I'll recover my spirits.

The smell bursts within me, bathes my brain with a salutary emanation. I can feel myself relaxing and all of me becoming larger at the same time − my heart, my arse and my ideas, above all my ideas. Everything becomes simple, simple and good. Wait, transvestite, I'll give it to you, your blow job; a really good one, you'll see! For a moment, you'll forget your torment of being a man, only half a one, it's true, but that's already a great deal too much. You'll bless Heaven for having given you balls, and perhaps, for a second at least, you'll regret having to mistreat them, like Chinese women had to do to their feet in past centuries. Forget the Elastoplast, transvestite, bandages are good only for mummies. And, you see, you haven't dried out yet. On the contrary, you're juicy, engorged with sap. It's a crime to hide away a bamboo cane like that. See it germinating, when I lick it, and growing even bigger. Come into my mouth, yes, right in, this time I'm properly in control. Ah! The tropical climate suits you? Hot and wet . . . Single-handedly, I'm making you your very own monsoon. I'm salivating on your prick with an abundance I didn't know I had. I've never had so much saliva. I'm becoming a swamp, you're sliding over my tongue like a long sampan, a scented junk, now harboured in.

So, you're suddenly less nervous, are you, my dear little girl? You're concentrating on what you're feeling. Isn't this a nice blow job? Wait, wait, it's not finished yet. The little ampoule has given me infinite inspiration, patience and power. I'm going to soak your balls, make them sticky, viscous, wet you all over and it'll soak right down into your soul, suck you with my whole mouth, my cheeks, like a big melting sweet, there, here, somewhere else, everywhere, I tell you . . .

Rub the end between my lips, enjoy the little sound of a damp cork popping out of the bottle, rub further in, rub the underside of your spear on the points of my teeth, further out, the cleft in your prick on the point of my tongue, further in, the whole shaft thrust in and the skin of your balls under my mouth . . . Can you feel yourself getting bigger? How lucky you are to be a man! What luck to have all that in your knickers so you can be brought off. You're made to be sucked, pumped, breathed in, drunk, suckled, chewed . . . It's a banquet in itself, your prick. Have you ever considered the fact that you're carrying a whole supermarket full of foodstuffs under your skirt?

In the vegetable department, there are all the things that are soaked, stood on end, tapered, dampened: leeks in vinaigrette, asparagus in a frothy sauce . . . Sisters, tonight we're having carrots. And they're still stiff. In the cold meats department, we're overburdened with stock. It's an orgy of sausages . . . I'm guzzling your pork sausage, browsing on your chipolata, swallowing your salami, whilst you're having your arse polished until it gleams. What a picnic!

And what about seafood? Did you know that I like underpant-eels, wriggling trout, joke gudgeons? With one flick of your fins, here you are again at the back of my palate, warming up my chin with your burning plums. Dessert already? Wait, let me organise it, I'm greedy but I'm refined: let me sweeten my coffee with a long sugar-stick, let me dip your biscuit in it, soak your bread in it . . .

To hell with the calories. I'm treating myself to a proper, first-rate feast. It's the euphoric moment when all the guests are replete and start fooling around. As for me, I'm going to smoke your cigar, pansy dressed in silk, pretty boy in a sheath-dress, buggered, in the same way as I will swallow the smoke like a big girl, without coughing. If you'd be so good as to serve me the liqueurs . . .

And with a loving, connoisseur's hand, I caress his balls, as you would dreamily stroke the side of a beautiful decanter of brandy with a promising nose. The surrealistic side of the situation is that I'm insinuating my fingers a little further in, and I'm touching another pair, yours in the circumstances, my darling, continuing to crush themselves rhythmically under her swelling buttocks, moving away only to press against them once again.

Four chicks with a single shake of the hand, a fine family! My left hand is overwhelmed by the four daughters of Dr Darche, and the right is clenched at the base of your John Thomas, whose tip is rubbing against my saliva glands.

The mouth-burner I'm meticulously giving him will soon be living up to its nickname. My jaws are stretched to the point of agony, my tongue is suddenly very tired, and still I'm sucking away at you. Tell me, guys, exactly when are you planning on doing your fair share? Not so much as a little squirt?

If I could just sniff another little dose of amyl . . . But it's no good dreaming of it, not in the present state of things, which I'm working away at with an understandable impatience.

It's just not true, this transvestite has terrible trouble in coming! OK, last straight line, I'm warning you, I'm beginning to lose patience. This time it's a devilish blow job, my hermetic mouth around your recalcitrant knob, my tongue and my palate like a vacuum cleaner, my lips like leeches . . . I'm going to suck your load out of you by force, you tight-arsed, constipated, dry-pricked bastard, I'm going to tear it out of your nuts, probe you, operate on you, bleed you white, you're going to shoot your load, by God!

Your prick must have doubled in volume, and I'm pumping away at it fit to suffocate myself; no one has ever bashed the bishop with as much faith, as much religion . . . Come on, you altar cruets, it's the moment of elevation. Talk about a mass! I'm giving you the blow job of the century, sucking your cock like it's never been sucked, I'm driving back your fire and unsheathing your lance at the same time . . .

Rabelais, it's really nice, extracting the marrow. And that's still to come. From this bone I've been gnawing at for nigh on a quarter of an hour, all that's flowing for the moment is a thin trickle of broth which mixes so intimately with my saliva that I don't know whether it's his juices or my saliva flowing . . .

I promise, I promise! This is the last of my Mohicans, never, never again will I scalp any, I'm smoking the pipe of peace. But what energy I'm putting into it: as I suck, my cheeks hollow and my neck swells up. I'm the frog – so, dollybird, who's the bull? I hope you've got something in your love-apples after all this, because the fruitlessness of my efforts is beginning to throw me into despair, as you can see . . .

No, even so, there's a justice in it, a moral; at school, I learned that perseverance is always rewarded. And here he is coming, the fancy-man, at a full gallop, shouting out loudly, stamping in the storm and singing in the pouring rain. Throwing back my stiffened neck, I catch sight of your hands gripping her breasts, and hers above, scratching you furiously, I glimpse her smooth, dark belly twisting in pleasure, and at last I receive her spattering joy, with my

173

incredulous throat which is splashed with three long fruitful spasms, accompanied by syncopated, musical, almost lyrical moaning . . . Sing, closet Amanda Lyre, soul in delirium, diva of the wardrobe, tragic castrato!

The only thing that remains is for me to hope that, behind her and in your turn . . . But I don't have the leisure to worry for long. I had forgotten that, apart from climaxing, this Marilyn with balls does everything very quickly. In one movement, she pulls away from my lips, separates herself from you, pulls down her dress, picks up her bag, which she had thrown away carelessly on a hook before the battle, bends to the ground and picks up the poor rag of her unusable misery-concealer, and almost instantaneously disappears with a pirouette and 'Bye! See you around.' This leaves us panting and standing staring at each other across the empty space which she has left between us, and slowly we return to reality, a process punctuated by the hissing sound of a toilet being flushed very near to our hiding place . . .

I hardly dare look at you any more. How much did you really see? How much did you glimpse of your unusual mistress, how much did you guess from her haste in turning her back on you, her haste to leave us? Didn't you feel, beneath your balls, a suspiciously-identical contact, didn't you feel at the moment of orgasm which made him thrust out his buttocks that it was an orgasm just like yours, the victory of an ejaculation which had long been desired, the triumph of the man who spurts forth at last, comes into the world and dies in the same second?

I don't know if you yourself came, and I haven't the courage to ask you. Your prick is still naked and poking out of your disordered clothes, and it's still stiff. But that's no proof, because I know it's stubborn beyond the honest average, and I have sometimes seen it, defying all the statistics, set off on another charge after a first rush without even pretending to weaken first.

But let's bet all the same that the adventure has tired you, for you seem a little stunned, a little slowed down. I'm still asking myself about your impressions, waiting for your

174

verdict, when – after a sigh (of regret? weariness? resignation at seeing the best moments ended?) – you at last smile at me and declare: 'She was good, wasn't she?'

Oh, yes, my darling, she was indeed good! Girls like that don't come along very often. But you can count on me not to be too free with my cheery confidences, and so dishonour the memory which you will keep of this pretty girl who stuck her bottom out for you. You two were beautiful together, and I remained in the shadows, humble and diligent, drinking at the bottle of misery, consoling, with my mouth and my hands, this splendid, moving half-breed, which an ironic destiny forces to hesitate between two colours, between two races, between two sexes, this siren distressed by her prick, this prisoner of a sole and tragic bar, this figurehead of a boat which casts off, but which is cruelly moored by an importunate cable . . .

My love, rock to yourself the pride of having possessed a creature of dreams, a vamp, a star, an unbridled mare, and leave me, without knowing it, to my pain of having done so little, of having been able to do so little, of having found beneath the poor bandage a throbbing abscess, and of having merely applied my lips to it, as one might seek to extract the poison left in a wound after a snakebite . . .

Come outside, my love, my man, my dear mate, come and breathe the night air, and the happiness of being two, and different, and made for each other. Come and make me love my femininity, your virility, and the ease with which they meet and overwhelm each other . . . Put your hand there, between my thighs, where it is hot, divided, wet, trembling, hollowed out . . .

Do you know that there are people who weep in the shadows because they haven't got that hole, that little button, that cleft?

Tell me – have you kept a little bit for me, too? Tell me. Will you take me here, in the street, against the wall? Yes, just there, in my cunt . . . I think I was born with this furrow, with this grotto so that one day I might know you, give them to you, and henceforth feel empty when you don't come inside . . . How delectable you are, this evening, and how you make me climax!

If I told you that you have taught me about my body, and the pleasure of playing with it, would you believe me? If I told you that I have never been so happy to be a warm, open, scented, easy woman, would you believe me then, too?

If I told you that . . .

EPILOGUE

It would be dishonest to deny that, in our story, there were some episodes that were much, much more indecent . . . Fucking in the cinema, the threesome and the anecdote of the masochistic gynaecologist are only amusing little trifles in comparison with what sometimes, with what finally and almost involuntarily we lived through . . . I say 'almost involuntarily' because it is obvious that in order to give ourselves to such extremes, we were so.

Taking our feet off the pedals and letting the beast within us all speak out, letting it express itself with crude words and salacious gestures, that's nothing, that happens to everyone. Becoming only one sex organ, one arse, burning and unrestrained, that's something very ordinary and very forgivable. But bringing the – I scarcely dare speak the word, but truth demands it, and absolve me if you can! – bringing the heart into these sorts of goings-on nevertheless arises from a damnable audacity, and from an obscenity at the limits of what is bearable, as I'm sure you'll agree.

And yet, I swear it, we had absolutely refused to do it, and what's more we laughed, as if we were conjuring up an event which was absolutely impossible. We had said 'No loving', just as we might have said 'No going to the moon'. Alas, alas, through trying to reach seventh heaven, through sending ourselves soaring up into the air, we sometimes almost landed on the moon, without even thinking of it, without realising it . . .

Those are the moments which I'm going to talk to you about today, at the cost of torturing your modesty and violating your memory which perhaps placed them back in the cupboard like a load of scandals you want to stifle. Believe me, I'm suffering too, so much so that I could cry out, all the more so because I am no less guilty, far from it. *Mea culpa*. I'm moving on to confessions now. And may you all remember that a sin confessed . . .

There were warning signs, and we should have taken heed of them. I remember that one day, after a really healthful and frenzied horseback ride – you had toiled away at me for a long time, and demanded that I should come a respectable number of times and I didn't think I ought to go against your wishes – we were getting our breath back, our bodies arranged carelessly, lying one against the other, and abandoning ourselves to the innocent pleasure of unimportant little confidences and conspiratorial teasing.

Suddenly, when I pulled a face, or perhaps said something which you found funny, you leapt towards me, very spontaneously, very vigorously, very new, and you took me into your arms. 'Ah, I do love you!' you cried. I buried my face in you to hide my turmoil. What you had just said then suddenly seemed to me to be very bold.

I struggled; I lectured myself. I demonstrated to myself that I was nothing more than a dirty slut with a vivid imagination, who saw evil where none existed, and that your exclamation, which had been sudden and without forethought, certainly resulted from a normal post-coital feeling of tenderness.

And yet, it sounded an awful lot like what people usually call a 'cry from the heart'.

For my part, it is true that already for some time I had been feeling myself weakening. I was not always a perfect mistress, and my preoccupations sometimes made me stray from the straight pathway which they should never have left:

178

the pathway which your prick traced out when it buried its stiffness inside me . . .

I had begun to dream of you, but can one be guilty of one's dreams? The horrible thing about it was that my dreams were not necessarily erotic. I'm ashamed to confess it, but more and more often I found myself thinking of you without masturbating, without even feeling the honest heat, the loyal shiver that the thought of a lover should evoke in his mistress's knickers. There was something else troubled inside me besides my cunt, something that I couldn't quite locate but which seemed suspicious to me. For as long as possible, I hung on to this abominable suspicion, and then, one day when I had a bad dose of the flu, with a fever which could excuse anything, I hung on to you and began to reveal the terrible truth. I had assuredly fallen very low, for slyly I had begun to love you . . .

Your tact and indulgence were perfect. You pretended to ignore this little bit of filth to which I had just abandoned myself. With a kind smile at the corners of your mouth, with calming gestures and few words, you cajoled me to make me shut my mouth . . . Finished, gone, away with the filthy words of a confession which one might regret! Washed away with a kiss, denied by a doubtful pout, the filthy little thing began to melt in the sunshine of your candour which, you will understand, much more easily lent itself to listening to my filthy delirium in passionate moments than to my sick words of love . . .

Strengthened by your example and by your rough treatment, I soon got better. 'You know, it was just a bad fever,' I said. Of course, you knew. You knew from instinct, you knew from experience, you knew in your heart.

After my transitory weakness, I promised myself that never again would I soil such a beautiful sordid affair with the triviality of my impure feelings, and I tried with all my strength to forget that there was within me a bizarre place – neither hole nor hair nor skin – which waited for you all the more eagerly when you had caressed, licked and overwhelmed all the others . . .

For what it's worth, I reconquered my innocence by some very Pascalian procedures. 'To believe in God,' said the Philosopher, 'kneel down and pray, and it will come of its own accord.' And so I began a perfectly conscientious re-education: no thinking of you except as a lover, which involved a whole series of spiritual and physical exercises. In this way, I trained myself to evoke your soul only with regard to its attraction for sexual fantasies, only the hoarsest, most disturbing tones of your voice, only the lewd flashes of light that yellowed your eyes. But in any case, it was better to imagine your body rather than your soul, your hands rather than your voice, and your prick rather than your eyes . . .

What's more, these fantasies were to be accompanied, whenever possible, with serious sacrifices to the most convincing onanism. And so I caressed myself a certain number of times whilst thinking of you, and my goal was eminently therapeutic. Through this I came to ask myself if I hadn't rediscovered the reflex of Pavlov's dog; you replaced the dog with a pussy, the bell with a Christian name – yours, under the circumstances – and you obtained the same result . . .

I was well on the way to recovery.

It was you who compromised everything. Yes! You! And the relapse was very severe, not to say definitive. One day, you decreed: 'I want to spend all night with you; I want to sleep with you!' and I felt a delicious little shock. Not that I had never thought about such an extravagance, but I had always been afraid that my whim might, in your eyes, appear to arise from some very vulgar affectation. In proclaiming 'No loving', we had in our own way erected barriers, invented taboos. 'No loving': didn't that also mean 'No senti-mentality'? Sleeping with me, you had said 'sleep', and that was a programme which was still forbidden, never realised, never even envisaged, and whose sudden perversity over-whelmed me.

To make our corruption complete, we had carefully set the scene. Neither the harsh light with which you usually liked to illuminate our antics, nor the complete darkness which

180

avoured the delirium of minds at the same time as the explosion of bodies, but the gleam from a candle, a dangerous deviation towards romanticism, towards intimacy, towards tenderness and gentleness. The brightness of its flame danced on us and made us more beautiful, more mysterious, more moving . . . We were not alone in the house, and the fragile partition walls, which were insufficiently discreet, forbade us to give in to the turbulence of our usual frolics. How could anyone not succumb to such a climate? A dusky gloom which warmed the amber flame of a candle without betraying it, and a muffled silence, peopled only by our whispers . . . Even less open people than us would have allowed themselves to be tempted . . .

I wanted you madly, and I thought at first that my body, this dear, solid, decisive companion, would monopolise both our attentions. It behaved like a hero, casting itself into the water to save appearances and drown the fish, striving, struggling, and climaxing very quickly, very quickly and very strongly, making me breathless and speechless.

But it was you who spoke. Ah, you should never have spoken. Your voice, in that warm, trembling gloom, your voice which was lower, more serious than on other days, and for once so easy, flowed naturally, like warm water . . . Not limpid water, though. A troubled, tormented, murky water, a current rising up from great depths and bringing with it spoils of torn algae, sand, broken shells, a hoard of secrets, a hoard of confessions, of confidences, and I listened to you, transfixed by stupor and immense gratitude . . .

Oh, the things it said! The things it said! We were swimming in full madness, you relating the state of your mind, and me drinking in your words with delight . . . Wasn't that becoming sordid?

Of course, the reasoning animals which moved within us soon got the upper hand again. And we wisely began to touch each other again, to embrace and caress. But our hearts were no longer in it. It was too much, you see. I gave myself to you with ardour, passion, abandonment. You asked for the most tender gestures, the most ardent surrenders from me,

181

and demanded them and commented on them with other words than those of your previous confession. But even those words, beastly, truculent, at last decent, made me melt with gratitude, for this was perhaps the first time that you had offered me so many words, so much eloquence, and the vocabulary you were using suddenly paid homage to me as it recalled my own words, those which I had sometimes murmured or howled at you, and which you had kept within yourself, and which you were now giving back to me transformed, metamorphosed by your voice of a man in love.

You took me often and everywhere, everywhere at once. You did your best not to leave anything in me that was not overwhelmed by your flesh, and I consented with terror to all your invasions, encouraged them, exalted them. You stepped through my narrow gate with an ease which surprised you. You whispered to me that I had never been so welcoming, and it was true. I felt I was deep, easy, permeable to all investigations.

Something within my being gave way without violence, without resistance, the barriers no longer existed, I could have taken you entirely into me . . . You had softened me, made me tender with your speeches, with your voice even more than with your great living body on which played the gleam of a flame, more than with your eyes shining in the darkness, more than with your hands on my skin . . .

Words sang in my head, mad words which peacefully mingled the most charming, the most naive love and bestiality, ordinary words and fantastic words . . .

My love, come, invade me, slide right into me, dwell in my arse as your only possible home . . . Come further in, further still. Come and thrust into the depths of me, come up against my retaining walls, work upon them, break them down, hollow them out. Why don't you come even more, come bigger, stronger, I'm a magic cave, thrust right into my secrets, into my treasures. Put your balls in me too, I want to feel them in me, full and throbbing, open me up, it's so easy, since I love you, and I have the right to tell you so . . . My mouth has still not confessed anything, but my body is shouting it out in its own way. My body is opening itself up for you as it has never opened itself up before. It's not your fingers, nor your gentle and terrible prick which have made me so wet, persuaded me like this. It's your words which have flowed into me, bathed me, soaked me all over, and I'm an immense gulf to overflow with you, and which will never be sated.

As you throb away voluptuously like that deep within my belly, you are going to make me fly far away, I can feel the ineffable caress of your balls on my buttocks, I can feel my heart exploding three times every second, and your marvellous proboscis smashing into me, and I am so willing, a gaping cathedral where your battering ram toils wildly . . .

That's it, that's it, it's coming, I'm going to tell you, I'm going to tell you that I love you, that I've loved you for so long, and so much, so strongly . . . I love you!

I told you, I told you, consciously, voluntarily, orgasms are no excuse, I offered this delectable abomination all on my own, I love you, and I will perhaps never again be able to climax without shouting it out again . . . I love you, I love you . . . Well, that's wonderful, great. What a mess, what a defeat, to have kept it in for so long, to have fought against it for so long, only to give in like this because of a miserable candle and you, becoming loose-tongued! I'm ashamed of such incontinence, ashamed but so relieved . . .

You possessed me again, you lay underneath me, relaxing, and I climbed astride you, my marvellous courser, and my mouth, next to your ear, continued its terrible story . . . Make yourself a place, my love, trace your path in me, I can feel you throbbing in my cunt like a captive bird, a very warm, very alive bird, dazzled by the trap into which it has just fallen. I shall keep you, I shall become your cage, your prison of flesh and blood, all the words which I speak will weave around you a tissue which will prevent you from struggling. Use your spear to pierce a tunnel into me, a tunnel where you would like to bury yourself forever and whose frontiers intoxicate you . . .

Place your hands upon me. You do not have hands to match

183

your trade. You have the hands of a mason, a blacksmith, powerful hands which will open me even more. Since I have known you, I can no longer be content with a single visit at a time, I want your fingers inside my arse, fashioning me, filling me up, working towards my painful, sovereign joy.

I want your mouth on my breasts, I want intense contradictions, my great one, my tiny child of a man who comes from my very entrails and returns to them as the salmon returns to the stream. I want to be your wife and your mother, I want to suckle you with an imaginary milk, a milk of tenderness and miracles.

I want you to hold me wide open, tearing me apart, I want your arms to hold up my thighs and I want your assault on me to be impetuous, deep, I want not to know if I am fucking or giving birth, if you are making me pregnant or being born from within me . . .

I demand paradox; I demand that you wait for me, that you keep your spunk inside you to the very limit of your powers, that you hold yourself in, that you hold back for a long, long time, so as to offer me pleasure for a long, long time, and I demand that you surrender, that you flow, that you ejaculate, that you spatter me, that you climax very quickly and very strongly, that you empty your balls with a cry of surprise and happiness, of regret and victory . . .

I want all of these proofs of love, and many more besides, the most ordinary, the most worn out, the most marvellous. I want you to masturbate in front of me, be a little ashamed of it, and I want your obedience to overwhelm me: I want to watch as your hand moves on your shaft, see the particular position of your thumb, meticulously controlling the movement, I want to see your grimace of concentration, your solitary fever which at the last moment casts itself towards me; you hang from my neck with your innocent hand, whilst the other henceforth escapes from your control in its frenzied race; you hang from my neck to invite me, to associate me, to thank me . . . How heavy you are at the moment when you come, how alive and magnificent you are, and how I love you for loving me enough to be simple, and a man, and to say: 'That's the first time I've done that for anyone . . .' Oh, what an intoxicating formula: 'the first time'! For among all my demands, among all my banalities, there is still one which is impossible, Utopian, intoxicating. To be the first, the first one somewhere for you, the first and the only one perhaps, the most, the least, the superlative, the one who eclipses all others with her presence and her words, with her love and her fervour . . .

The night is not over and we still talk incoherently for a long time, henceforth resigned to our sad fate as debauchees who love each other. The candle burns, the symbol of an eloquent fragility, but, protected from the wind, it keeps tenaciously alight . . . I burn with it and my flame is no less fervent. You are still speaking, and there is a celebration in my heart. You speak and you move me, with your simple words devoid of promises, with your passé phrases, and with your touching care never to conjure up the future . . .

The sole vision of the future which you proposed to me has remained engraved on my memory like the most overwhelming of all your confessions. 'You mustn't blame me if one day I go away . . .' And I accepted from you, from you alone, what would have wounded me if it had come from another; more than just accepting it, I savoured it . . .

To anyone else, my offended sensibilities would have replied: 'And why shouldn't I be the first to leave?' But, coming from you, I knew exactly what the formula meant, and it intoxicated me to analyse it.

For it was a declaration which you were making me there, no doubt about it. A very daring declaration, a way of suggesting: 'And if, one day, I loved you to the point of danger, if I loved you so much that we had to split up?' This thought, worthy of Napoleon who said: 'In love, there is only one form of heroism: flight', this imperial, delicate thought, this way of confessing and recanting at the same time remains for me a jewel without price, the engagement ring which you would never offer me, the non-proposal of marriage of a man who feels he is on the edge of passion, yet is preparing himself never to give in to it.

185

That is how I understood your words; that is how tha
prayer has remained in my eyes the most extraordinary thing
you have ever said, the most torrid moment of our libertine
novel . . .

No, my tender lover, I shan't blame you, you are free in
what you do, in your soul and in your heart, free from your
anxieties and your scruples, free also from all remorse, for
I would have this stoicism, if it was necessary in order to
please you, to swear like Cyrano at the moment of his death
'No, no, my dear love, I didn't love you!'

And you took me again, to conjure emotion, that
formidable go-between. You held me tighter, closer to move
further away, and you made love to me as though to unmake
it, as soon as you had confessed it. Pleasure came easily to
me, that night. I ran, flew, danced in your arms, like a little
mad dog, like a Brazilian woman possessed by the samba,
like someone pursued by an uncertain peril.

I fled from you, too, I denied your power even though it
had only just dazzled me, and I worked hard at ignoring you,
at deriving pleasure only from your imperious prick, from
your hands which had suddenly become more skilful, from
your skin which slid against mine, from your mouth which
was so bountiful in its kisses and open-sesames, which made
me open myself, burst forth and surrender . . .

But, alas, at the moment of joy, my tongue betrayed me,
speaking your Christian name, which up until then I had
always been able to hold back . . . Impetuous as a runaway
horse jumping a fence, your Christian name gambolled off
into the night, and never again could I bring it back, reduce
it to silence. As sly as a prisoner on the run, it has often risen
to my lips since then, always at moments when my vigilance,
dozing with pleasure, was unable to prevent it.

And we fell asleep, so miraculously fitted together in that
narrow bed, two perfectly fitting pieces of the same puzzle,
companions suddenly broken off from everyday demands.
The experience ought to have been new, and yet I had this
strange feeling that I had always shared your sleep, and of
knowing instinctively what position to take in order to adapt

186

myself to your big body and not disturb it. I uncovered you as you slept, modest and kind, attentive to my wellbeing as I was to yours, and I thought perhaps we shouldn't have. I had to retain the image of him awake, peremptory, sometimes egocentric, turbulent. Now, I thought, I'm going to love him also because he's sleeping, and because his sleep is even more touching than all the rest. You see, I had just touched the very depths of pornography, of horror, of the unspeakable . . .

Dawn's light caught us unawares, tired, troubled, as though we were bewildered by the adventure. You left without many words, and suddenly I had the immense hope that it was nothing, that the past night belonged to a sort of intoxication for two in which we had rambled in convoy, and where we had been exalted more than was allowed . . .

When I next saw you, you had a distant quality, a little lukewarm, a little flighty. Oh! scarcely, but already so much too much! As suffering awakened within me, alive, keen, throbbing, I understood that I could make a great cross from my hopes of recovery, a heavy, painful cross. Alas! The diagnosis had suddenly just become precise, in a luminous and irremediable way, from the too-obvious symptoms of my doubt, if your eyes seemed to flee from me, and my pain, if they settled on another woman . . .

I tried to consider the truth directly. It was serious, very serious. A tumour which was perhaps not incurable, but in any case malign. Worse than a cruel abscess but soon burst, a real sickness, insidious, slow-developing, caught through imprudence, through inadvertence, through naiveté. A sickness of the heart, one of those you always think only happen to other people.

I breathed very hard, and decided to live like this, with this shameful and well-hidden sickness, this leprosy, this cancer, this waterlily in my chest, which stifled me a little, but which no one could see, which those around me were still unaware of: my love for you.

You did not pass through my life without leaving any trace. You are the father of this child, the only one which we shall ever have together, which – line after line, page after page – I am bringing little by little into the world, and which you called up, evoked, suggested . . . Your fatherhood, like all fatherhoods, is limited to that single role of fertilisation, and I'm accomplishing the rest with seriousness, with fervour, with the pain and the pleasure of working for a long time and choosing my words, my phrases and my sentences before giving birth alone to our joint work: a child of love, a child of paper, made out of your semen – the memories which you left me, the dreams which you inspired in me – and born out of my faithful labour, my writer's confinement. The paper child of a paper woman . . .

I dedicate it to you, in memory of our adventures and our wanderings, as the token of a love which never surrendered to the traps of daily life, and which, when it became too sincere, preferred abnegation to banality . . .

This is for you, then, man with yellow-gold eyes, my forbidden love, whose enthusiastic prick and bashful tenderness will long haunt the memory of this paper woman . . .

HELP US TO PLAN THE FUTURE OF EROTIC FICTION –

– and no stamp required!

The Nexus Library is Britain's largest and fastest-growing collection of erotic fiction. We'd like your help to make it even bigger and better.

Like many of our books, the questionnaire below is completely anonymous, so don't feel shy about telling us what you really think. We want to know what kind of people our readers are – we want to know what you like about Nexus books, what you dislike, and what changes you'd like to see.

Just answer the questions on the following pages in the spaces provided; if more than one person would like to take part, please feel free to photocopy the questionnaire. Then tear the pages from the book and send them in an envelope to the address at the end of the questionnaire. No stamp is required.

THE NEXUS QUESTIONNAIRE

SECTION ONE: ABOUT YOU

1.1 Sex *(yes, of course, but try to be serious for just a moment)*
Male ☐   Female ☐

1.2 Age
under 21 ☐   21 – 30 ☐
31 – 40 ☐   41 – 50 ☐
51 – 60 ☐   over 60 ☐

1.3 At what age did you leave full-time education?
still in education ☐   16 or younger ☐
17 – 19 ☐   20 or older ☐

1.4 Occupation _____

1.5 Annual household income
under £10,000 ☐   £10–£20,000 ☐
£20–£30,000 ☐   £30–£40,000 ☐
over £40,000 ☐

1.6 Where do you live?
Please write in the county in which you live (for example Hampshire), or the city if you live in a large metropolitan area (for example Manchester) _____

SECTION TWO : ABOUT BUYING NEXUS BOOKS

2.1 How did you acquire this book?

I bought it myself ☐   My partner bought it ☐
I borrowed it / found it ☐

2.2 If this book was bought ...

... in which town or city?   _____
... in what sort of shop: High Street bookshop ☐
local newsagent ☐
at a railway station ☐
at an airport ☐
at motorway services ☐
other: _____

2.3 Have you ever had difficulty finding Nexus books on sale?

Yes ☐   No ☐

If you have had difficulty in buying Nexus books, where would you like to be able to buy them?

... in which town or city   _____
... in what sort of shop from list in previous question   _____

2.4 Have you ever been reluctant to buy a Nexus book because of the sexual nature of the cover picture?

Yes ☐   No ☐

2.5 Please tick which of the following statements you agree with:

I find some Nexus cover pictures offensive / too blatant ☐

I would be less embarassed about buying Nexus books if the cover pictures were less blatant ☐

I think that in general the pictures on Nexus books are about right ☐

I think Nexus cover pictures should be as sexy as possible ☐

SECTION THREE: ABOUT NEXUS BOOKS

3.1 How many Nexus books do you own? _____

3.2 Roughly how many Nexus books have you read? _____

3.3 What are your three favourite Nexus books?
    First choice _____
    Second Choice _____
    Third Choice _____

3.4 What are your three favourite Nexus cover pictures?
    First choice _____
    Second choice _____
    Third choice _____

SECTION FOUR: ABOUT YOUR IDEAL EROTIC NOVEL

We want to publish books you want to read − so this is your chance to tell us exactly what your ideal erotic novel would be like.

4.1 Using a scale of 1 to 5 (1 = no interest at all, 5 = your ideal), please rate the following possible settings for an erotic novel:

Medieval/barbarian/sword 'n' sorcery ☐
Renaissance/Elizabethan/Restoration ☐
Victorian/Edwardian ☐
1920s & 1930s − the Jazz Age ☐
Present day ☐
Future/Science Fiction ☐

4.2 Using the same scale of 1 to 5, please rate the following styles in which an erotic novel could be written:

Realistic, down to earth, set in real life ☐
Escapist fantasy, but just about believable ☐
Completely unreal, impressionistic, dreamlike ☐

4.3 Would you prefer your ideal erotic novel to be written from the viewpoint of the main male characters or the main female characters?

Male ☐ Female ☐

4.4 Is there one particular setting or subject matter that your ideal erotic novel would contain?

_____

SECTION FIVE: LAST WORDS

5.1 What do you like best about Nexus books?

_____

_____

5.2 What do you most dislike about Nexus books?

_____

_____

5.3 In what way, if any, would you like to change Nexus covers?

_____

_____

5.4 Here's a space for any other comments:

_____

_____

_____

_____

_____

_____

_____

Thank you for completing this questionnaire. Now tear it out of the book – carefully! – put it in an envelope and send it to:

Nexus Books
FREEPOST
London
W10 5BR

No stamp is required.